# A Prophecy: Book 2

# A Prophecy: Book 2

## The Chosen Hybrid Series

Sharuthie Ramesh

Copyright © 2016 by Sharuthie Ramesh.

| Library of Congress Control Number: | 2016904635 |
|---|---|
| ISBN:     Hardcover | 978-1-5144-7761-8 |
| Softcover | 978-1-5144-7762-5 |
| eBook | 978-1-5144-7763-2 |

All rights reserved. No part of this book may be reproduced or transmitted in any form or by any means, electronic or mechanical, including photocopying, recording, or by any information storage and retrieval system, without permission in writing from the copyright owner.

This is a work of fiction. Names, characters, places and incidents either are the product of the author's imagination or are used fictitiously, and any resemblance to any actual persons, living or dead, events, or locales is entirely coincidental.

Any people depicted in stock imagery provided by Thinkstock are models, and such images are being used for illustrative purposes only.
Certain stock imagery © Thinkstock.

Print information available on the last page.

Rev. date: 04/18/2016

**To order additional copies of this book, contact:**
Xlibris
1-888-795-4274
www.Xlibris.com
Orders@Xlibris.com

# Dedication

For my parents; my inhumanly beautiful mother
who loves me too much and my wise father whom
I get my wits from; they are my anchors.
For my aunts and uncles who are always
on my side of the argument.
For my grandparents who have been
pampering me since day one.
For my cousins who have put up with me since 2000.
For my friends who listen to my wacky ideas
And still hang out with me.
For the bookworms.

# Contents

| | | |
|---|---|---|
| Chapter 1 | A Big Problem | 1 |
| Chapter 2 | The Prophecy | 6 |
| Chapter 3 | Arguments | 10 |
| Chapter 4 | Unexpected | 15 |
| Chapter 5 | Bigger Problems Arise | 19 |
| Chapter 6 | Trouble | 24 |
| Chapter 7 | Prisoner | 29 |
| Chapter 8 | The Servic Wolf Pack | 33 |
| Chapter 9 | Rescue Team | 38 |
| Chapter 10 | Back to the Castle with Surprises | 43 |
| Chapter 11 | Breakfast with Friends and Foes | 49 |
| Chapter 12 | The Infirmary | 57 |
| Chapter 13 | The Meeting | 67 |
| Chapter 14 | Another Deatheye | 74 |
| Chapter 15 | When Riddles Are Revealed | 84 |
| Chapter 16 | Issues | 94 |
| Chapter 17 | Visitors | 103 |
| Chapter 18 | Farewells | 112 |
| Chapter 19 | Confessions and Memories | 124 |
| Chapter 20 | Family Problems | 135 |
| Chapter 21 | Long Talks | 147 |
| Chapter 22 | The Sisters | 157 |
| Chapter 23 | Aftermath | 165 |

# CHAPTER 1

## A Big Problem

EVERY TIME I thought I could finally live in peace, I was proven wrong. First time was when Aries Deatheye asked me to marry one of his sons. I agreed, and a year later, when I got married to Gustav Deatheye, I thought I could finally live in peace with a spouse. Unfortunately, I was proven wrong when my dead ex-boyfriend and killer stepped back into my life. This time, I'm going to tell you a story about a prophecy that came with more than one problem. It started a few minutes after Siddiqis Starburn showed up.

I was in the greater living room of the castle, with an icepack on my head. I glared at Siddiqis, who was also holding an icepack to his head and staring at me. Gustav, my husband, was glaring at Siddiqis as well, wanting to kill him. But if he killed him, I'd die as well. Siddiqis and I were a whole, thanks to the new prophecy:

"The Sinner must take his place beside the Chosen Hybrid, for both are a whole." If he got hurt, I got hurt. If he died, I'd go down with him. The Sinner and the Chosen Hybrid were Siddiqis and I.

Gustav groaned with impatience. "Where's Angela?"

I sighed. "She was at her sister's birthday when she was told that my ex-boyfriend was back from the grave and I'm connected to him. Cut her some slack."

It was 3:30 p.m., and Angela was all the way back in the Mortal Portal, enjoying her little sister Althaea's birthday party. I felt bad to pull her out of the party, but I also needed her to explain.

I heard the front door of the castle open and slam shut, and a second later, the living room's door opened with a bang. Angela Scarblood stood in the doorway, eyes green as a cat's. "Where's the devil?"

Siddiqis smirked slyly. "Hello to you too."

Angela stared at him, a stunned expression on her face, and then she turned to me with brows furrowed. "What are you doing here?"

He spoke in his familiar sarcastic tone. "I'm chilling in my ex-girlfriend's castle." Then he scowled. "What do you think I'm doing here? I'm here to ask for help."

Angela walked into the room, and that was when we all noticed the girl behind her. Her hair was long and dark, her skin a light golden shade. Her eyes were a bright gold.

I knew her in an instant. "Why'd you bring Althaea here? She shouldn't be worrying about these things!" I scowled at Angela, who scowled at her little sister.

"I told her to stay back, but she wouldn't," Angela explained, glaring at Althaea. "Also, she can help."

Althaea was 116 years old, and Angela was her guardian. Since their parents died in the war that killed mine, Angela and Althaea had no one. Angela was the eldest Scarblood, so she was in charge of her little sister.

Althaea stared at Siddiqis. "Is this he?" she asked, her gaze not leaving him.

Siddiqis smiled sweetly at her, like he was peering at a child. "I'm Siddiqis Starburn. You must be Angela's little sister, the weakest link."

All of a sudden, Siddiqis threw back his head with a cry of pain. He held his head, and before I could react, I felt a piercing pain in my head, as if my skull was cracked open. I shouted in pain. As sudden as it came, the pain stopped. I looked up to see Siddiqis, who was still recovering from the pain. I stared at Althaea, whose hand was raised in front of her.

She lowered her hand and stared at Siddiqis with cold eyes. "I'm more powerful than you think, and I'm much stronger than I look. Don't test me again." She then looked at me, concern in her eyes. "I'm sorry. I had to know if it was true."

I nodded understandingly, and I rubbed my temple as I felt a headache emerge.

Angela glared at Siddiqis, who was rubbing his temple as well. "Althaea isn't a death angel like me. She's a powerful dark angel, meaning she's as powerful as you and I. Maybe even like Kyra."

Gustav groaned in frustration. "Angela, just help us."

Angela turned to Gustav. "I can't help you," she admitted, "but she can." She jabbed a thumb at Althaea, who was expressionless.

Siddiqis snorted and smirked at Althaea. "You're kidding, right? No offense, sweetheart. You may have some powers, but this is a crisis made by Heaven. Sure you can handle that?"

Althaea stayed expressionless. "Angela is a death angel, meaning she can read the Book of Prophecies to see if it's true. But I'm the one who can see how we can unconnect you two."

I nodded. "Althaea, did you bring the book?"

"Yes and no."

Angela sighed. "In order to summon the book, you and Siddiqis have to join hands and chant."

Siddiqis stood up and walked over to where I sat. I stood, and I was hesitant. But I bravely held out both of my hands in front of me, and he took my hands in his, sending shivers of disgust up my arms. His magenta eyes were piercing through my soul, and I stared into them with courage.

Siddiqis turned his gaze to Angela. "What do we say?"

Angela spoke in a solemn tone. "The Sinner and the Chosen Hybrid, two parts of a whole, hold a question for the book that knows." Her green eyes flashed. "Repeat that until the book appears."

We nodded, and Siddiqis turned his attention back to me. I nodded, and we started to chant, our voices in harmony, his lower and mine higher. "The Sinner and the Chosen Hybrid, two parts of a whole, hold a question for the book that knows. The Sinner and the Chosen Hybrid, two parts of a whole, hold a question for the book that knows. The Sinner and the Chosen Hybrid, two parts of a whole–"

All of a sudden, a great golden ball of energy appeared above Siddiqis and me, as it generated the Book of Prophecies. We stared in fascination as the book appeared and rested on our joined hands. The golden ball of energy was gone, and the Book of Prophecies was here.

# CHAPTER 2

## The Prophecy

ANGELA TOOK THE book carefully, and Siddiqis and I unlinked hands. The book was eye-catching. Its golden cover shone with the dust of angelic power. The silver accents covered the spine delicately, and the words The Book of Prophecies lay on the front cover. We all stared in wonder at the book.

Finally, Angela spoke out loud to the book, "Book that knows, what is the present prophecy?"

The book's cover flew open, and several pages passed until the book stopped on one page. On the top was "The Sinner and the Chosen Hybrid."

Angela translated the angelic writing that said the prophecy. "The Sinner must take his place beside the Chosen Hybrid, for both are a whole," she said in a solemn voice.

I heard Gustav curse. Siddiqis grimaced at the truth, and I stared at the book in shock. I really was connected to him.

Angela turned to her little sister and gestured for her to take the book. Althaea took it carefully and took in a deep breath. "Book that knows, show me the words that no soul can see."

A page flipped on its own, and Althaea read it silently, eyebrows scrunched. Finally, she exhaled and chose her words carefully. "Well, every prophecy must be fulfilled. But this prophecy is different, since Kyra was able to fulfill the last one. In order to fulfill this prophecy, we need to break the connection."

Siddiqis stared at her, waiting for her to continue, but when she hesitated, he scowled. "Do you want to tell us how?"

She looked uncertain. "Let me check again." She looked back down at the Book of Prophecies, eyes full of concentration. We were all silent for her. Finally, she looked taken aback and continued to reread a sentence. Then she looked up at me. "This doesn't make sense."

I walked over to her and looked at the page. It was blank to me, but I knew there were words that only she could see. "What is it?"

She looked at Angela; confusion clouded her eyes. "This doesn't seem right."

Angela stared at her sister. "Explain."

Althaea started to shake her head. "Yes, it can be fulfilled, but there's a big risk involved."

Gustav got off the sofa. "I don't care! We just want the connection broken. That's why we are all here." He stared at Althaea with impatience.

She bit her lip. "Do you all really want to know what the book says?" she asked, eyes flashing toward Siddiqis and me.

Siddiqis stared. "Tell us."

I nodded. "Please tell us, Althaea."

She took in a deep breath and looked down at the page. "'To fulfill the Sinner and the Chosen Hybrid prophecy, the connection must be broken by the hands of Death. Then Karma will fulfill the deed.'" She looked up at Siddiqis and me and saw our confused expressions. She sighed. "I think it means both of you must die."

I felt as if a wave of cold water washed over me, and I knew Siddiqis felt it too. Gustav stared bewildered at me, and Angela looked stunned. I took in a long and slow breath. "So let me get this straight. Siddiqis and I have to die in order to break the connection?"

Althaea stared at me, unfazed. "I'm so sorry. It's the only way."

All of a sudden, Gustav ran past me and pinned Althaea to the wall, knocking the book out of her hands. The book disappeared into thin air, back to Heaven. She didn't fight back, only stared at him with flaming eyes.

Gustav seethed at her, eyes filled with blinding rage. "There's got to be another way! Tell us!"

Angela stepped toward him, eyes full of protection for her sister, but Althaea shot her a look that told her to stay where she was.

Althaea glared at him. "I told you all I know."

"Liar!" He snarled.

Althaea's eyes blazed into a bright golden and started to mutter in the demonic language. Suddenly, Gustav stepped away from her, clutching his head in agony. He shouted in pain and went to his knees.

I ran to him and knelt beside him, cradling his head in my lap. "It's all right, it's all right." I looked up at Althaea, eyes blazing. "Stop, Althaea, stop it!" I shouted, my voice echoing.

Finally, she stopped, and Gustav relaxed against me, breathing deeply as if he had been running forever. I whispered soothing words to him, trying to ease the pain. I looked up at Althaea, who was expressionless. "Why would you do that?"

She smirked. "You really do love him. I thought he'd be stronger than that, but I guess he really is weak."

I scowled at her. "He's not weak. He has a heart."

Hurt flashed on Althaea's face.

I softened up. "Althaea—"

Before I could finish my apology, she was out the door, and I heard the castle's front door slam shut, leaving the trail of steam behind her.

# CHAPTER 3

## Arguments

I FELT HORRIBLE about what I said and instantly wished I could've taken it back.

Siddiqis sighed. "And then there were four."

Angela peered down at me sympathetically. "It's all right. She'll forgive you sooner or later."

I still felt terrible. "I forgot that she's a dark angel. Oh my god, I feel awful." I held my head down in shame.

Gustav frowned. "It's my fault. I shouldn't have insulted her. I feel bad too."

Siddiqis groaned. "Please, can we all just stop feeling bad? Right now, I'm still linked to Rumblen."

I glared at him. "Don't call me Rumblen. You lost that privilege when you killed me. The first time." I added venom to my tone for good measure.

Siddiqis stared at me, expressionless. "Holding that against me, are you?"

"Oh, yeah. Definitely. One hundred percent yes," I said, scowling. I stood and walked toward him. "By the way, you still haven't mentioned why you're here."

He smirked. "I missed you."

"Is it opposites day already?" I snorted. "Spill it, Starburn."

He stared at me intensely, eyes blazing. "I'm here to kill you."

I didn't step back; in fact, I stepped forward. I narrowed my eyes, and I got it. "But you can't kill me because of the prophecy, so you came to find out how to break the connection."

Siddiqis smirked. "Smart girl. Now we have to break the connection."

I laughed shortly, but it was humorless. "We? You're kidding, right? I'll never work with you."

His magenta eyes blazed down at me. "I don't care. We need to break this connection."

I smirked. "Now why would I want to break the connection? It's the only thing keeping you from killing me. This is my leverage."

He loomed over me, but I only smirked. I wasn't afraid of him anymore. Siddiqis stared down at me, a horrible glint in his eyes. "You will help me, or else I'll kill everyone you love and know." He smiled as my smirk faltered.

I narrowed my eyes at him, feeling their colors intensify. "Excuse me?"

He grinned wickedly. "Listen, babe. You either help me, or your husband loses an arm. Both arms if you piss me off."

I stared revolted at him. "You wouldn't dare." Then it took me a while to register the fact that he had called me babe. I shook it off though.

He lowered his head until our faces were merely inches apart. His breath reeked of blood. He grinned darkly. "Try me." He whispered.

We stayed there like that, staring each other down. I felt like shoving him into the wall again, but the last time I did so, I felt the pain as well. I glowered at him instead. He looked like the old friendly Siddiqis I knew: tousled short dark-brown hair, slightly golden skin, lean and muscular body, and magenta eyes that gleamed brightly. But I knew that he was evil. His eyes were still magenta, but they were cold and vacant, showing that he had no soul. No heart.

If I were a cartoon character, smoke would be blowing out of my ears. "Keep my friends and family out of this." I seethed.

Siddiqis smiled coldly and cocked his head slightly to the side. "No can do. You see, your friends and family are my leverage, while this connection is yours. If you say you won't help, one person you love drops dead, and then another, and then another." His eyes flashed wickedly. "You get the point."

Without thinking, I grabbed him by the collar of his torn leather jacket and pulled him down until we were face-to-face. "I swear to God. You touch my friends, and I will send you to Satan myself."

He peered into my eyes, his gaze mocking. "Do it then. Kill me. Protect your loved ones. Take stab at it, sweetheart." He spread his arms out, gesturing for me to take a shot at him.

But I wasn't dumb. "I would kill you right now, but I don't want to end up with the devil." I let go of his collar and stepped back, crossing my arms in front of my chest.

He grinned. "Thought so. Now give your word that you will help me break this connection." His eyes were so taunting and lingering.

I stared at him. "No."

He grinned as if pleased. "All right then." His gaze travelled to Angela and then lay on Gustav. "Whom should I start with?" His eyes flashed. "Let's start with the dark angel who brought you back to life."

Siddiqis lunged at Gustav like lightning, pinning him to the wall. His hands were around Gustav's neck in an instant, and Gustav started sputtering, clawing at his hands.

Suddenly, I felt fear for Gustav, and I automatically ran at Siddiqis and pulled him away from my husband. I tossed him into a wall without thinking and instantly regretted it the second I felt a pain in my side. I fell to my knees, clutching my side, and I looked up to see Siddiqis doing the same thing. I kept my face down, trying to mask the pain from my face. Gustav knelt down beside me, worry crossed over his face. Angela rushed over to Siddiqis, hands outstretched in case he recovered before me. I peered into Gustav's blue eyes and felt my pain ease away. After a minute, I got to my feet with the help of my husband. I saw he had bruises around his neck, a sign that Siddiqis had hurt him a lot.

I turned to see Angela, hands still stretched out, glaring at Siddiqis, who was now recovered but on the ground. Angela spoke in a low voice that could have been mistaken as a growl. "Stay down."

Siddiqis glared up at her, eyes narrowed, and he was muttering in a different language. It was familiar, but I couldn't grasp the memory. Then I realized what he was doing. Before I could warn Angela, her body shook as if she were struck by lightning, and she collapsed to the floor, limp.

# CHAPTER 4

## Unexpected

I SCREAMED. THE lights flickered, the door opened and shut, the floor shook, and the windows shattered from the sound. Gustav tried to reach for me, but I was already kneeling beside Angela's limp body. I held two fingers at her wrist and exhaled when I got a pulse, though it was faint. Her chest rose up and down slowly. I held my hands on her chest, over her heart, and closed my eyes, concentrating on giving Angela strength. I felt some of my energy slip through my hands and sink into Angela, restoring some of her energy. Then I took my hands away and waited.

Finally she opened her eyes, their colors more vivid than ever. I exhaled in relief and held her hand, gripping it firmly. Angela peered up at me as if waking up from a long nap. "What happened?" she croaked.

I looked at Siddiqis, and then I felt my worry turn into full on rage. "Get out!" I shouted at him.

He flinched at the sound and slowly got to his feet, staring at me with an expression I couldn't read. He walked to the door, and Gustav took the opportunity to go with him and make sure he didn't murder anyone. Gustav turned around before he left, and I nodded. With that, the door closed, and it was just Angela and I alone. I was breathing hard as if I had been running forever.

Angela stared up at me calmly though she was also slightly ashamed. "Siddiqis is stronger than I thought. I can't believe he was able to take me down."

I sighed. "He's stronger. We need to find out how to break this connection, and fast." Siddiqis was going to be a problem, especially because if he did die, I'd go down with him in an instant.

Angela nodded, and after a minute, I helped her up to her feet and told her to rest in a guest room. Even though she refused, I told her that I'd feel safer if she stayed, and so she stayed for my sake. I decided I needed some time to myself to think. I walked out of the room while Angela called Althaea to tell her she was staying in the castle overnight, and I grabbed my leather jacket.

"Gustav?" I shouted.

Automatically, I got an answer. "Yeah?" he shouted back, the sound echoing.

"I need to clear my head. I'm going to the park. If you need me, I'm there!" I hollered as I trudged on with the jacket.

"You're the princess! Just stay safe, Rumblen!" he hollered back.

"Okay, I'll be back soon!" With that, I opened the front doors to the castle, and the fresh, cool spring air hit me delicately. I sighed at the scenery, the now growing flowerbeds and greenery, and I made my way to the park. As I walked down the trail, I noticed that everything was fine; nothing alarming was in place.

After five minutes of walking down the trail, I arrived at the park. It was a beautiful grassy area with a few flowerbeds and a playground. I walked over to the wooden bench for two and sat alone, taking in the peaceful setting. I wished every day was going to be peaceful, but unfortunately, Siddiqis had to come back into my life. I inhaled the sweet aroma of flowers and grass and exhaled deeply. It seemed like the perfect moment.

"Remember me?"

I whirled around on the bench to face the person behind me. It was a girl, my age. I had a feeling that I knew her but just couldn't place her name. Her denim jeans were ripped, her tank top was blue but stained with dirt, and she was wearing blue sneakers. Her hair flowed over her shoulders and down her back, wildly, and her skin was golden. Her eyes were a bright green, marking her as a werewolf. But I got another vibe from her. That was when she smiled, and I saw her fangs. She was a newly turned vamp but also a werewolf–a vampwolf. She looked as if she was on the run from something. There were rarely any vampwolves in Xercus, so I stared at the stranger with caution, in case she was a rogue one.

"I'm sorry. Have we met?" I asked, trying to place the name on this familiar face.

The vampwolf smiled; her fangs peeked out. "C'mon, Kyra. I dated a certain warlock."

Just like that, I grinned with surprise. "Laylita?"

Laylita Howls grinned as well. "So you do remember me?"

I jumped off the bench and embraced my old friend. "Of course I do! How could I forget my favourite werewolf?" Laylita Howls was one of my old buddies back in the Mortal Portal Academy. She was a werewolf with attitude, and she dated Aleks Silvermoon, my warlock buddy, but they broke up after the war. "Why haven't I seen you around? Where have you been?"

Suddenly, her face went serious. "I need your help. I've got a big problem."

I was taken aback by how serious my jokey friend was. "What's wrong?"

"I got bitten by a rogue vamp, and now I'm a vampwolf!"

I sighed. "Yeah, the fangs explain it. Did you tell your parents?"

Her eyes were frantic, full of worry. "I did, but they threatened to send me to the Wolf Council, where I'd be killed! So I ran away."

I swore. "Laylita, you can't just run away! The Wolf Council will look for you. You have to give yourself over to the Vampwolf Clan so you won't be considered a rogue!"

Laylita looked like she was hiding something. "Here's the thing. What if I told you there's this werewolf?"

Uh-oh. "What do you mean?" I stared at her, trying to understand what she was saying.

Laylita suddenly started to cry. "Kyra, I messed up!"

I felt fear for my friend. "Laylita, what did you do?"

She looked up at me, a look of helplessness on her face, and I knew something was terribly wrong, but I didn't see what was coming. "I'm pregnant."

# CHAPTER 5

## Bigger Problems Arise

I FELT AS if someone had punched me, like all the air in my lungs was sucked out. I didn't know what to say. A pregnant vampwolf was a rare occasion; I had never known any pregnant vampwolves before that moment. If Laylita went to the Vampwolf Clan and told them she was pregnant, they'd kill her and the baby. She was in deep trouble. Being a pregnant vampwolf meant being a disgrace to both races.

I took in a shaky breath, looked down, and listened. I heard faintly the beating of a child's heart. That's when I noticed the roundness of her belly. A bump. A baby bump. "Laylita, who's the father?" I dared to ask, hoping it was a close friend instead of a werewolf stranger.

She stared at me with regret. "His name is Stefan Darkwoods, an alpha wolf. We dated after Aleks and I broke up, and when I was bitten and became a vampwolf, we made love. I thought that cuz I'm part vamp, it would be impossible for me to get pregnant, but afterward, I missed my period and got cravings for more blood. I used a pregnancy test, and it came out positive." She shook with shame.

I hugged my friend lightly and wondered what to do. I couldn't take her to the Vampwolf Clan; they'd kill her. "When are you due?"

"In a month," she mumbled.

I swore. I already had to deal with the connection problem, and now my friend was in danger. I drew away from her and held her at arm's length, looking her in the eyes as I spoke in a strong voice. "Laylita, you have to listen to me, all right?"

She nodded, still sobbing silently.

"No one can see you. You can stay in the castle where it's safe. I'll get you a pregnancy test, and when you give birth, I'll get a doctor that I trust to help you give birth. You can't tell anyone you're staying with me. Right now, I have another big problem on my plate, so we might have people come to the castle. Don't let them see you. Your safety is my priority."

She sniffed. "No, Kyra. I can't stay with you."

I was bewildered. "What do you mean?"

"I'll put you and Gustav and everyone in trouble. If the Vampwolf Clan finds out that you're harbouring a pregnant vampwolf–"

"They won't find out," I interrupted. "You'll be in the castle, and no one can enter without permission, especially not a vampwolf. I'll protect you."

"Kyra, you don't understand! If you take me in, he'll follow me."

I scrunched my eyebrows in confusion. "Who?"

Laylita looked around; we were alone. "Stefan, the werewolf. When he found out that I'm pregnant, he wanted to tell the Wolf Council. I ran away from my pack, but a week later, he found me and almost killed me. I hid in the woods where he thought I wouldn't be, and I've been on the run for about eight months now. The pack, the Vampwolf Clan, and the Wolf Council are looking for me. I needed to find someone to help me, but Aleks probably wouldn't help. He'd probably slam the door on my face, and my werewolf friends will just turn me in. Then I heard that you and a Deatheye prince got married and you were in Xercus. So I got here as fast as I could, and here we are."

I took a moment to register what she had just said. "Okay," I said slowly. "So the father of your unborn child wants you dead?" I shook my head. "I really wish this happened with you and Aleks, then I could have a serious talk with him. What does this werewolf look like?"

She stared at some children that were on the swing set. "He's intimidating. He looms because of his height. He has broad shoulders. He has a golden tan, dark hair worn short, and light gray eyes. That's how I saw him last, but if he changed, he can be recognized by his alpha wolf ring. He never takes it off."

I nodded in thought. "All right. C'mon, let's get to the castle."

Laylita groaned. "He'll find me, Kyra. I don't want him to hurt you or—"

"Laylita Howls, I'm the most powerful hybrid. I can handle a crazy werewolf."

She appeared startled. "What do you mean?"

I stared at her, stunned. "You weren't told?" The look on her face explained. "I'm the Chosen Hybrid everyone's talking about, and Siddiqis is the Sinner."

She stared, awed. "Oh my god, I should have known! And Siddiqis is evil? Seriously?"

I sighed. "Being on the run meant no news, eh?"

"Yep."

"All right then, I'll fill you in when we get to the castle. Right now, we need to go." I grabbed her hand.

"Hello, ladies."

Laylita and I jumped at the voice and whirled around to see a man older than us, dressed in jeans and a plaid shirt, and his dark-brown hair was gelled back. His eyes were shielded by his tinted shades, and he wore an egocentric smile, charming yet intimidating. He was slightly tanned, a perfect crispy golden color. But his arrogant vibe annoyed me. Though I felt the need to put this stranger in his place, preferably a trash can, I decided to be polite.

I smiled. "Hello. I'm not sure we have met."

He grinned. "Indeed we haven't. But that doesn't mean I don't know the princess when I see her. Those killer legs of yours gave your identity away."

Flattery was not the best way to make an acquaintance with a married woman. I introduced myself anyways. "I'm Kyra Rumblen Deatheye. And you are?"

"A young man wanting to help. I've overheard you two ladies saying you two are headed to the castle, and I'd be happy to give you two a ride." He grinned his best-selling grin, but it had no effect on me.

Though that didn't mean I was willing to walk, especially since walking meant more people would see Laylita. I nodded, trying to look comfortable even though the stranger was staring to creep me out.

He gestured to a Jeep. "Ladies."

We both climbed into the back, and the stranger got into the driver's seat. As we drove to the castle, I couldn't help but feel something wasn't quite right. My hybrid senses started to tingle; they only tingled when it meant people around me were in danger.

It was then I realized we were heading in the opposite direction of the castle.

## CHAPTER 6

### Trouble

"UM, YOU'RE GOING the wrong way," I said, trying to keep the nervousness out of my tone.

He grinned and peered in the rearview mirror at me. "Actually, there's been a change of plans, my dear."

Suddenly he stopped driving, and when I opened my mouth to speak, he got out of the Jeep. Laylita and I exchanged looks. What's going on? I wondered with a frown. I got out of the Jeep, and so did Laylita. I looked around to see we were in the middle of a grassy plain, a forest just a mile away. The kingdom was out of sight, and we were all alone. Not my favorite scenario.

I whirled around to face the stranger, who was grinning evilly. "What's going on?" I asked in a superior tone.

He advanced upon Laylita and me, and I reflexively stepped in front of Laylita; the urge to protect her pounded in my ears. He grinned even wider. "I needed to get you two alone. No one can find you two here. No one can hear your screams."

I was about to ask him what was he talking about, when my gaze slipped to his hands. On his right hand, a silver ring shone in the sunlight. It had a wolf on it. It struck me what that ring was: an alpha wolf ring.

Uh oh, I thought. It was a trap. I pushed Laylita even more behind me. "Laylita, run."

She started running for her life, heading toward the woods. The stranger went to chase her, but I blocked his path in an instant. "Leave my friend alone," I said in the coldest voice I could do, but on the inside, I shook with adrenaline.

Stefan Darkwoods smirked. "I can't do that. I need to kill that vampwolf who's harbouring my mistake."

I stayed in his way. "You're going to have to get past me if you want her."

His eyes twinkled with mischief. "All right." He swung his fist at my nose, but I caught his fist midway.

I squeezed his fist, satisfied when I heard the crunching of his bones. "Big mistake, pal." I hooked him in the jaw with my other hand, and he fell to the grass. I kicked him several times in the stomach and jumped on top of him, hands around his throat. He growled and shook his body wildly, trying to shake me off. But I had a strong grip, and being a hybrid, I was definitely stronger.

I levelled my face inches above him. "This is what you get for messing with a pregnant vampwolf and her hybrid friend."

To my surprise, he laughed. "You think a wolf travels alone. No, we travel in packs."

Before I could react, strong arms pulled me off Stefan and threw me down to the grass. I squinted up at the figure, and my heart dropped. There were several werewolves, all male and all tough-looking. Two of them grabbed my arms and heaved me to my feet with superstrength. I struggled, trying to get free, but their grips weren't normal.

I glared at a smiling Stefan. "You think your little friends scare me?"

He was on his feet, and he strode toward me. He stopped when we were inches apart. I held up my chin in confidence as he slowly lowered his face closer to mine. He's breath smelled like animal blood, and I urged myself not to shiver. "No, but they're here to help me. Bring her."

I saw behind him two werewolves dragging a screaming Laylita. Her eyes were full of fear, and I struggled to get free. As the two werewolves released their grip on her, Stefan turned and instantly had a hand around her neck. Laylita's lips started to turn blue, and I knew in a few minutes, she and the baby would die.

"Let her go!" I shouted, trying to break away from the two werewolves' grip.

He looked at me, still gripping Laylita's neck. "I need to get rid of her. Don't worry. I'll get to you next."

"Please, you're the reason she's pregnant! That's your child she's carrying! Let her go! I'll give you anything you want, just let her go!" The words slipped out of my mouth in a rush.

Stefan gave it a thought and then loosened his grip on Laylita's throat. Her colour was returning, but she was still so weak. "What do you mean?"

I swallowed and spoke carefully. "Whatever you want, you'll get. Just let her live." I shook, trying to stay calm and talk it out without getting Laylita killed.

Finally he let her go, and two werewolves grabbed her arms so she couldn't leave. Stefan turned to me and gripped my chin with his thumb and index finger. I stared up at him with confidence he hated.

He stared down into my eyes through tinted lens. "I want you to come with me as my prisoner, to my pack, to show everyone I was able to bring down the great Kyra Rumblen Count." He spoke in a low voice, and his tone chilled me to the bone.

I stared at him, stunned. My plan had backfired. I should have known he'd ask for such a thing; he wanted to be known as the powerful werewolf. I wished I just took back whatever I said, but then Laylita would die. I had to make a choice. I decided that her safety was more important. Besides, I would find a way out of this mess.

I heaved in a breath. "Fine."

He smirked. "Give me your word."

"What?"

"I said, give me your word." He sighed. Then he snapped his fingers, and the werewolves holding Laylita started dragging her to the Jeep.

I panicked. "Fine, fine! I give you my word!"

He grinned and spoke to the werewolves but stared at me the entire time. "Take the vampwolf to the castle. I'll take care of the princess."

Laylita started screaming, "No! Kyra, don't! He'll kill you!"

I stared at her, urging myself to wear a brave face, and smiled weakly. "I have to, Laylita. I swore to protect you. I'll be fine. Don't worry."

If only I was able to convince myself the same thing.

# CHAPTER 7

## Prisoner

I WATCHED THE werewolves drag a sobbing Laylita to their Jeeps and watched them ride away, to the castle. It was only the two werewolves, Stefan, and me, along with two other Jeeps.

Stefan spoke. "You two, go back to the pack. I'll meet you guys there. Dismissed." He addressed the two werewolves, and they released their grips on me and rode away in one of the Jeeps. It was now just the werewolf and me.

I grew tired of the silence. "What are you going to do to me?" I dared to ask; the suspense was killing me.

Stefan eyed me and came so close to me our bodies touched. I felt very uncomfortable, but I wasn't a fool to let him notice. But my heartbeat must have given it away, because he smirked. "I'm not going to kill you, if that's what you're asking. I rather break down that annoying confidence of yours. But I must say, you are rather noble to your friends."

"I'd give up anything for Laylita."

"Even your life?"

I raised my chin and looked him straight in the eye. "Anything."

He seemed surprised, but he quickly hid it. He reached into his jeam's pocket and retrieved a duct tape.

I laughed. "You're kidding, right? You really think duct tape is stronger than a hybrid?"

He laughed as well, to my dismay. "Of course not! This is enchanted." He grinned at the way my eyes widened. Then he went serious. "Hands behind your back. Now."

I scowled at him but did as he said. For all I knew, Laylita may have still been with those werewolves, and I wasn't taking chances. Stefan walked around me, to my back, and started duct-taping my wrists together. I stayed still as he worked, and finally, when he was done, I couldn't help but try to free my hands. It was useless; it really was enchanted.

I faced him. "Now what?"

He cocked his head. "Now we go to my pack in Servic. Get in the car."

I obeyed, and I sat in the backseat, glaring at him as he slammed the door and sat in the driver's seat. I really hated him. I really need to talk to Laylita about her choices in men, I thought, and then I realized that I wouldn't come back. I was a prisoner.

We drove in silence, and finally, after five minutes, I spoke. "You know my husband's going to find me and kill you, right?"

Stefan smirked and peered at me in the rearview mirror. "I'll be more than happy to take down your husband in front of your eyes."

I laughed, though it was humourless. "As if you can take on a dark angel."

"Actually, your husband isn't as strong as he was before. Now he has feelings that make him weak. I can kill him in my sleep."

His arrogance was annoying. "You must feel pretty damn good about yourself right now, don't you?" I was disgusted.

He grinned. "Pretty damn great, actually." Then he stopped the car and got off. He opened my door, and I glared at him as he pulled out the duct tape roll. He ripped off a piece. "Sorry, but I need some peace and quiet." He placed the strip over my mouth, and I felt my glare intensify. He smiled and then slammed the door shut. He climbed back into the driver's seat and started driving again. I wanted to say some unintelligent words, and the piece of tape on my mouth wasn't enchanted. But I kept quiet, trying to think of a way to escape.

I thought and thought, and finally it hit me. Siddiqis. I was able to connect with him now that we were bound more than ever. I closed my eyes and focused on sending my soul to Siddiqis. As much as I hated having to see him again, he was my only chance of being saved. Finally, after a minute, I felt my soul drift out of my body, and I peered at my body. Then I flew out of the Jeep and headed to the castle.

When I got there, I saw no sign of the werewolves' Jeeps. I floated right through the door and gaped at the scene in front of me.

Gustav and Laylita were hugging and crying, Siddiqis was staring off into space, and Angela was on her knees, face covered in her hands. It was as if I had died again, and they all must have thought I was going to die soon.

I couldn't take it anymore. I jumped in front of Siddiqis. "Siddiqis Starburn, do you hear me?" I yelled.

Siddiqis jumped at the sound of my voice and stared at me. Then he tried to hug me, but passed right through me. He went pale. "Oh my god, you're dead, aren't you?" Then he looked confused. "Wait, if you're dead, then how–"

"Listen to me! I'm not dead! I sent my soul out of my body so I can talk to you. Tell the others I'm here."

He turned to Gustav and the others, who were staring cautiously at Siddiqis. "Kyra's here."

Gustav glared at him, but confusion clouded his eyes. "Don't play games with me, Starburn."

Siddiqis shook his head. "Kyra sent her soul here to contact us."

I nodded. "That's right. I'm here, Gustav and–"

Gustav stared ahead, waiting. Everyone now had their eyes on Siddiqis, waiting as well.

"They can't hear me," I realized out loud.

Siddiqis stared at me. "Where is that werewolf taking you?"

"To Servic, to his pack."

"I know where they are then. We'll be on our way. And, Kyra?"

"Yes?"

"Don't ever put your life in danger." He was dead serious.

I left the castle without saying a word, allowing Siddiqis to tell everyone where I was. I focused on my body, and then I was suddenly in the car. I went into my body and heaved in a breath through my nose. I opened my eyes to see Stefan's face inches away from mine.

# CHAPTER 8

## The Servic Wolf Pack

I SWORE UNDER the tape that was still over my mouth. I stared up at him, shocked. He looked angry. Uh-oh. A pissed werewolf was a scary werewolf. "What were you doing?"

I looked down at the tape on my mouth.

He sighed and ripped the tape off my mouth.

I winced at the sharp pain. "I was sleeping."

"People breathe when they sleep."

"I'm a hybrid, which means I'm half-vampire, meaning I don't breathe when I sleep." I felt a déjà vu, and a memory of Aries popped into my mind.

"I think you were calling for help." He glared at me through tinted lens.

I really wished he took off those glasses. I stayed calm. "I was sleeping," I repeated.

He gave me a look and then pulled me out of the car, into the crisp, fresh air. We were in front of an abandoned building, which was the Servic Wolf Pack headquarters.

I stared up at the wreck and then at Stefan. "So we're here?"

"Yep, we're here." He didn't sound happy or sad. He pushed me toward the building, and we walked in through a gaping hole, which was where the door should have been. The inside was like a hotel, a really old, run-down hotel. The carpet was stained with dirt and blood, the floor was dusty, and a chandelier was in the middle on the floor, when it should have been hanging instead. It felt musty.

I looked around and then at Stefan. "Where's the pack?"

He looked around, ignoring me. Then he let out a high-pitched whistle, and the pack came running down the dusty staircase.

They were all in human form, thankfully. Male and female werewolves came to a halting stop a few meters away from where Stefan and I stood, staring at us with shocked expression.

I raised an eyebrow. "So this is the Servic Werewolf Pack. It's been a while since I've visited a pack."

Stefan stared ahead. "Where's my father?" he addressed the group.

One male werewolf stepped forward. "He's in a meeting with other pack leaders."

Stefan pushed me forward. I walked through the crowd of werewolves. Each one stared at me, and I marched up the staircase, Stefan breathing down my neck. When we got there, he gestured for me to turn left, and I did. He stepped in front of me and opened the first door on the corner. We stepped in, him in front of me.

Inside, a meeting took place. I didn't know any of the pack leaders that were there, and I took a moment to take in my surroundings. The room was exactly like the one in Xercus, and there was a mahogany table in the middle. Sitting around the table were some of the pack leaders. Each one turned to look at Stefan and me, glaring. When they saw who I was, their expressions turned shocked.

The man at the head of the table stood up as we barged in. His dark-brown hair was short, his muscles rippled through his business suit, and he was also golden tanned like Stefan. The resemblance was quite frightening.

Mr. Darkwoods spoke in a superior tone that boomed throughout the room. "Stefan, what do you think you're doing?"

Stefan bowed. "Father, I've brought proof of my honour." He pushed me forward, so his father would see what he caught.

I smiled at Mr. Darkwoods. "Hello, Darkwoods. You and my parents were friends, correct?"

He stared at me, shocked. Then he turned to his smug-looking son. "What is the meaning of this?"

Before Stefan could talk, I piped in. "Darkwoods, your son has performed an act of treason. I hope you are aware how this makes your pack look like to others."

He glared at Stefan.

Stefan smiled, not realizing the glare was meant for him. "Father, you told me to come back with my honour, and I have. I have brought pride–"

"How dare you say you have brought pride and honor with you?" His father sneered.

The look of disbelief on Stefan's face made me smile. "I don't understand, Father," he said.

Mr. Darkwoods crossed the room in four strides and came to a halt in front of me. He gazed down at me. "I'm so sorry–"

This ticked me off. "Are you serious? Your son threatened to kill my friend as well as tied me up with enchanted tape, which is illegal for a werewolf to carry, and drove me all the way here, and you expected me to just simply forgive you?"

He turned me around and ripped off the tape from my wrist in less than a second.

I whirled back around to face the pack leader and rubbed my sore wrists. "Now that's better."

Stefan was red with rage. "Father–"

Mr. Darkwoods raised a hand, silencing him. "Not another word, young man. I'm very disappointed in you. Kyra Rumblen Deatheye is a respected leader, and you dare say you are higher than the Chosen Hybrid?" At the sight of my confused expression, he looked at me. "Everyone here is aware of your title."

I nodded absently.

The pack leader turned back to his son. "You have no right doing this. Kidnapping an official higher than you and keeping illegal enchanted tape? This is way out of the line, boy. You are to report to your room, where you will serve out your grounding."

"But–"

"Not another word." He turned to address the men behind him. "The meeting will be rescheduled. For now, I must escort Mrs. Deatheye back to her castle before anyone becomes alarmed."

Uh-oh. "Darkwoods, there's something you need to–"

Before I could finish the sentence, the room's door crashed inward. A figure stood in the doorway, hands braced on either side of the doorway. My heart skipped a beat.

"Hello, gentlemen."

# CHAPTER 9

## Rescue Team

Gustav looked so handsome and sophisticated in a tux. His dangerous side really brought out the danger in his cold light-blue eyes. His hair was ruffled, and he stood confidently.

When he stepped into the room, I saw he wasn't alone. Siddiqis and Angela took their place beside Gustav. Siddiqis was ordinarily scary, so the tux he wore really did enhance his complexion, and his magenta eyes danced with danger. He didn't look as if he had died. Angela looked tough in her battle gear—open black leather jacket, black tank top, black leather accent tights, black combat boots, and a belt loaded with weapons. They looked like a crime-fighting trio, with Gustav in the middle and the other two on either side of him.

I smiled and ran to Gustav. He swooped me into an embrace; his strong arms secured me like a wall made of stone. I took in his minty smell and the warmth of his body. We broke away and he peered into my eyes. I couldn't explain the love I saw in them; they were wordless yet held such a desirable meaning.

He cupped my face in his hands, inspecting my face with worried eyes. "Are you all right?"

I nodded.

Siddiqis took this as the perfect opportunity to confront the leaders of the wolf packs, who were staring at him in horror. He stepped in front of Mr. Darkwoods, who was disturbed. "Hello, I see you have all thought that I was dead. But let's set that aside and focus on what Mr. Stefan Darkwoods have done, shall we?" His taunting smile was a signature move, very lazy and intimidating.

Mr. Darkwoods straightened up. "Mr. Starburn, I don't think it was necessary to kick open my door. I hope you have the money to pay for that door."

Gustav cut in. "That was me, actually. You kidnapped my wife, so I felt it was fair to break it open."

Siddiqis scowled. "I don't care about the door. Your son is a disgrace to werewolves everywhere! He kidnapped the Chosen Hybrid, blackmailing her to get her to go with him. Your son has demonstrated an act of treason." He spoke in a strong voice that boomed through the room.

Mr. Darkwoods was expressionless. "I know my son has made a big mistake, and I guarantee that he will be grounded–"

"Please take this offensive, because grounding him is a stupid punishment." Siddiqis interrupted, earning a scowl from Gustav. You never, ever, say something rude to a wolf pack leader. Never.

Mr. Darkwoods turned a raging red. "Then what do you suggest, Mr. Starburn?" He held venom in his voice. Oh boy. This wasn't going to be good.

Siddiqis turned to me. Uh-oh. "You were the damsel in distress. You decide."

I ignored the first remark, and I let go of Gustav to face Stefan, who was expressionless. I gave it a thought and came up with a good decision. "Stefan Darkwoods, I've decided that you must come back to Xercus with me and live in the castle with Laylita Howls, the vampwolf that is harbouring your child. You must stay until the child is born, then you will have the choice of either leaving the child and Laylita or staying with them as a family. This is what I have decided. If you deny, I'll see you in court where you will be found guilty and be given a death sentence."

Stefan stared at me with a stunned expression. I was happy with the deal, assuring my friend's safety. Finally, he spoke. "All right, I accept. But I must be given three days—"

Gustav made a sound, resembling a growl. It was low and deep, but its message was clear: cooperate, no buts, no arguments. I loved him for that.

Stefan hushed up, nodded, and stayed silent as the pack leaders silently left through the broken door. They all gave me a good stare before they left, and in five minutes, we were alone with Mr. Darkwoods and his maniac son.

Stefan finally spoke. "When do we leave?" His voice came out like a rumble of thunder.

Siddiqis glared at him. "Go pack your bags and report to the front of the building in ten minutes. Go." His words sounded like a threat, each one dripped with venom.

Stefan nodded and then rushed out of the room. There was silence. Then Mr. Darkwoods silently exited the room without a word, leaving my friends and me alone.

I broke the yielding silence. "How'd you guys know where I was?" I then realized I should have been saying "Thank you," but I couldn't help but wonder how they were able to find me.

Angela smiled. "Believe it or not, your ex-boyfriend was actually of some use. He knew where the Servic Wolf Pack stayed, and he knew where to go." Her bright green eyes lit up with surprise as she realized what she had just said.

Siddiqis smirked. "It's funny how you all think so low of me."

Gustav and Angela turned to him, gawking. "You tried to kill us!" They shouted in unison as I shouted, "You killed me once and almost killed me again!" But then I softened up, remembering that he did come to save me. "But thank you," I mumbled.

Siddiqis looked startled. "What did you just say?"

It killed me to say it louder. "I said, thank you."

"For what?"

I sighed. "For coming to my rescue, even though you want to kill me."

His irresistible lips parted and then closed. Then he spoke quietly. "I owed you."

Now I was confused. "What do you mean?"

He stepped forward and shrugged, a naked look in his eyes. "You broke my curse, triggered the prophecy that brought me back, and here I am. Also, I did kill you, so yeah. We're even."

Something bubbled up inside me. It wasn't rage; it was . . . I couldn't explain it. It felt as if a part of me was lightened up. I didn't even understand why. I cleared my throat and looked away. "We should go to the front of the building." I couldn't look at him for some reason. Was I blushing? I hoped not.

Siddiqis nodded, but I knew he saw my expression, and he hid a smirk. It was hidden, but I saw its meaning: "Blushing for the devil?"

I realized that I was. And I hated that I was.

# CHAPTER 10

## Back to the Castle with Surprises

WE WERE AT the front of the building, waiting for Stefan to show up. After eight minutes, he appeared with his luggage. He was wearing what he wore before, except his glasses were off. His eyes were a piercing gray, very haunting. I mentally shuddered at their gaze.

Stefan glared at me. "Let's get this over with."

We all got into Gustav's Jeep and rode back to the castle in silence. When we got there, everything looked fine. We got out of the Jeeps and entered the castle. I didn't know what to expect, but it definitely wasn't what had happened.

Boota and Darq Deatheye were waiting in the front, both wearing a big smile on their faces. It appeared they hadn't seen Siddiqis. Boota beamed at the sight of me. "Kyra! We wanted to surprise you guys, but one of the servants said that you were out, so we decided to—" It was then that she looked over my shoulder and saw Siddiqis standing behind me, a smirk on his face. The look of horror on Boota's face was award-winning, considering she was scared to death in reality.

Darq's happy expression turned into a look of horror when he saw my suppose-to-be-dead exboyfriend standing beside me.

Oh boy. "Guys, I'm so happy to see you two. But I see you haven't heard about the new prophecy," I said, my lips pressed in a thin line.

Boota stood frozen. She pointed at Siddiqis. "K-Kyra, I-I think I-I'm going nuts." She always stuttered when she was embarrassed or scared; in this case, her stutter came out of fear.

I turned to face a smirking Siddiqis, and then I looked back at her. "Boota, you're not going crazy. Siddiqis really is here. I brought him back without even knowing."

Darq was pale. "Kyra, are you telling us that you brought back your evil boyfriend from the dead?"

"Um, if I say yes, what will you do?"

He raked a hand through his tousled hair. "I'd probably try to kill him." Then he looked at Gustav. "Why aren't you killing him?"

Gustav sighed. "If he dies, Kyra dies." Gustav explained everything that had happened, and afterward, Darq and Boota stood like statues.

Siddiqis stepped forward. "What are you two doing here?"

Boota scowled at him, though fear was in her eyes. "We wanted to tell everyone that I'm due this month." She absently rubbed her now big stomach, as if to sooth the baby inside.

I squealed with glee and ran to her, embracing her lightly. "That's great news! Congratulations!"

Gustav went to pat his brother on the back; Darq beamed with pride. Darq and Boota were going to be the best parents. Though chances were that they were going to spoil their child, the baby would be good. If the parents were good, so would the child.

Angela was jumping from one foot to another, and she was suddenly beside Boota. "Oh my god, oh my god, oh my god! Soon a little Darq will be born! This is so awesome!"

I broke the embrace to beam at Boota. "I'm so proud." Then I turned to Angela. "Can you help Boota to Aries's room? He won't be back for a while, so the two lovebirds can stay there."

Angela nodded and carefully led Boota up the stairs, to Aries's room. Darq trailed behind them, not letting Boota out of his sight.

When they were gone, I saw Laylita come down the stairs, and when she saw Stefan, she stopped dead in her tracks. Her eyes widened, and when she opened her mouth to scream, Gustav ran past me in a blur and covered her mouth.

"Don't scream. He won't hurt you. I promise. I'm really tired of people screaming now days."

She nodded, and he removed his hand from her mouth, and Laylita took in a deep breath. She looked at me. "Explain please."

I nodded. "I will. Gustav, can you show Stefan to his room? As far away from Laylita's room, please?"

Gustav nodded and came to me to give me a quick kiss. He turned to go, Stefan following him, but someone had banged on the front doors.

I walked to the front door and pulled it open. When I saw who was there, I was speechless. Then one thought registered in my head: Uh-oh.

"Hey, Kyra." Aleks Silvermoon's eyes flashed, and he grinned his old goofy grin. Usually, I'd be happy to see my old warlock friend. Unfortunately, with the current situation, I was in for it big time.

"Aleks. I didn't know you were coming," I said, staring at him like an idiot. My luck was crappy today.

He frowned. "I thought you'd be happy. I mean, it's been a whole year since we've seen each other!"

I sighed. "You haven't heard, have you?"

"Heard what?"

I pushed open the door more, and he slipped in. He actually changed. The short boy with wild hair now stood before me as a 119-year-old stranger. His hair was now short and light brown, and he was now an inch taller than I. His golden catlike eyes glowed brighter than before, and he was actually quite fit. This was not the scrawny, loner boy I went to school with. This was a grown man that worked in a bar and had striking features.

The second Aleks's eyes landed on Laylita, he was surprised. He was even more surprised to see her round belly. Then he frowned. Emotions filled the air.

Finally, he spoke in a low voice. "Please tell me this isn't what it looks like."

Laylita shook her head; remorse was in her voice. "Listen."

Aleks closed his eyes, brows narrowed in focus. It was dead silent, and we all heard the beating of a heart coming from Laylita's stomach.

When Aleks opened his eyes, they were filled with shock and guilt. "Please don't tell me I did that. I'm not ready to be a dad." He blurted out.

This got us all surprised. I was the first to speak. "Wait a minute. What do you mean? You two–" I covered my mouth with my hand in surprise. This was a shocker. And from the look of the others' faces, they didn't know either.

Laylita turned beet red with embarrassment. "No. This happened way after me and you."

Aleks was then just shocked. "So you had sex with someone else?"

"Yeah."

"Oh." He looked uncomfortable. "Well, this is awkward."

That's when Stefan decided to speak. "Who are you?"

Aleks narrowed his eyes at Stefan. "I'm Aleks Silvermoon, Laylita's ex-boyfriend. Who are you?"

Stefan scowled. "I'm Stefan Darkwoods, Laylita's ex-boyfriend as well."

This shocked Aleks, and when he spoke, his voice was uneven. "You're the father of the child?"

He looked down at his feet, not saying a word, but the silence was deafening.

Aleks sighed. "I guess that answers that."

Siddiqis was annoyed at the fact that Aleks still hadn't noticed him. "Hello, Aleks, old buddy. As much as I've missed you, can you leave?" He spat the words old buddy out as if they were poisonous.

Now Aleks stood as if petrified by fear. But that was soon replaced with an angry expression. Siddiqis and Aleks used to be best buddies. Now they were staring each other down, just like how you'd stare at an enemy.

Aleks spoke. "I'm not going anywhere until I know that everyone's safe. Meaning, I'll be going to find a room here in the castle."

Siddiqis glared at him. "Fine. But stay out of my way." Then he turned and walked up the stairs, turning the right corner to his former room, which he must've taken up again.

There was a lot of tension in the room, and I couldn't take it. "All right, I'm sorry, everyone, but I'm going to my room to sleep. Aleks, your old room is already waiting for you. Gustav, can you take Laylita to her room and Stefan to his room? I need some time alone." With that, I ran up the stairs and went into the master bedroom, my bedroom. I closed the door and sagged into a chair. Oh, how I was so tired. It had been a long day, and I decided to rest. I changed out of the dress into my favourite yellow tank top and slipped under the blankets in only a tank top and underwear. Gustav never minded my choice of pyjamas over the silk gowns. I closed my eyes, and before I knew it, I drifted off into a deep sleep, dreaming of a place with no problems.

# CHAPTER II

## Breakfast with Friends and Foes

I WOKE UP to the sound of knocking. I felt Gustav's warm arm around me under the blanket and heard his steady breathing. He wasn't going to get up, and I wasn't about to wake him up. He deserved to sleep in. I looked at the clock beside our bed. It read 7:30 a.m. Breakfast was at 9:30 a.m., as usual, so it was peculiar that someone was awake at a time like this.

I got off the bed, slowly so I wouldn't disrupt Gustav's sleep, and padded to the door, yawning. I opened the door and froze.

Siddiqis stood there in the doorway, shirtless and in boxers.

Dear god, help me, I thought as I stared blankly at him. Think of a blank sheet of paper. I think nothing of his body.

"Good morning, princess," Siddiqis greeted, his eyes flashing as he shot me a dazzling smile.

A blank sheet. No looking at his abs. You are married! I cleared my voice. "You know I hate formalities."

"Yes, one reason why I called you princess, babe." His smirk was annoying even though it still had me plummeting on the inside.

"Siddiqis, I'm a married woman. Call me babe again, and I'll rip out your eyes. Even if that may make me blind by doing so," I spoke coldly, narrowing my eyes.

He chuckled. "You still wear a tank top and undies to bed."

I looked down and realized that I was just wearing that. I turned red with embarrassment, but then I recollected myself quickly. "Do you mind? I need to get changed. Today's a big day."

He grinned. "You kicking me out, sweetheart?"

Ugh, the nicknames aren't going to stop, are they? "I'd feel better talking to you covered up," I admitted.

"Oh please. If I see something I haven't seen before, I'd throw a quarter at it." He smirked again at my disgusted expression.

"Good-bye, Starburn."

I tried to close the door, but Siddiqis was faster. He pulled me out of the bedroom, into the hallway, and closed my bedroom door quickly but silently. He backed me against the wall across my bedroom door and trapped me with his body, his elbows on either side of my head.

I tried to scream for help, but he covered my mouth. He motioned for me to be silent. Then he pointed at my bedroom door and motioned slicing his throat. I glared at him but nodded. I didn't want him to hurt Gustav.

He spoke slowly in a low voice, but his words were precise. "I don't have any intention to hurt your husband. But tell him about this, and I'll make sure he dies. Understood?"

I nodded, glaring daggers at him now. I fought to get free, but he pinned my hands above my head in one hand, covering my mouth with the other, and his body kept me pressed to the wall. There was no way out. He was stronger than before, which was scary.

He smirked. "Fighting won't help you, sweetheart. Listen to what I say. I may be linked to you, but let me assure you that once this link is broken, I'll be happy to end your life again, permanently. So you stay on my good side. Got it?" He had that scary gleam in his eyes.

I nodded again, trying to keep my anger down.

He released me, and as soon as he did so, I pushed him away and walked into my bedroom, slamming the door shut behind me.

Gustav jumped out of our bed, awake and shirtless. I forgot that he was sleeping. He appeared at my side in an instant, looking worried. "Rumblen, what's wrong? Why are you out of bed?"

I wanted to tell him, but Siddiqis's threat still rang in my ears. "Nothing. I just thought I heard something. It was nothing, really." I forced a smile. It hurt to lie to him, but it was for his own good. He'd do the same for me.

Gustav nodded and embraced me tightly, taking away all my worries. "All right then. I guess since we're out of bed, we might as well get ready for the day ahead." He gave me a kiss on the cheek and went to take a shower.

I yawned and then opened my bedroom door once more to make sure Siddiqis wasn't there. When I saw he wasn't, I let out a sigh of relief and closed the door. After slipping on a tank top and some jeans and using the bathroom after Gustav, I was ready for breakfast with my friends and foes.

Gustav and I waltzed out of room, arms linked. We walked down the hall, our castle staff greeting us. When we got to the dining room, we opened the doors to find our friends sitting at the table. Aleks was talking to Angela, Laylita with Siddiqis, and Stefan sat quietly.

When we closed the door, they turned their heads and saw it was us. Aleks was the first to speak. "Well, it took you long enough."

I smiled. "Good morning to you too, sunshine."

He grinned his old goofy grin on his new manly face. He was wearing a black T-shirt and old jeans. His hair was wet, glistening like fresh dew on grass. My old goofy, clumsy friend was a man. He was unrecognizable now.

I took my seat across Gustav, beside Angela. Angela was wearing a yellow flowing dress, and she had her hair down. She had grown it. Gustav clapped his hands twice, just how his father had done a thousand times, and in came the servers with plates full with food.

We all ate in silence. Then Aleks broke the silence. "So when is Aries coming back?"

Gustav cleared his throat. "He's supposed to be back in less than a week."

"How do you think he'll react to everyone being here?" I piped in, suddenly realizing that Aries had no idea our friends were all crashing at the castle, which was still his.

Gustav stared off, thinking, and then looked at me, horrified. "I have no idea, but something tells me it won't be good."

We all groaned in unison while Siddiqis muttered, "Just great. That's just great."

We all stared at Siddiqis. Then I spoke. "Siddiqis, you do know that when Aries sees you, his first instinct will be to drive a knife through your heart, right?"

Siddiqis looked at me. "Kyra, you do realize that when he stabs me, it'll be lights out for you too, right?"

I hated how he was right. "Looks like we've got work to do if we are going to break this bond."

Siddiqis grinned. "You actually said we. I guess that means I'm in, eh?"

I scowled at him. "Even if you didn't want to be in, you don't have a choice."

He raised his glass of orange juice at me, and I shot him a third-finger salute.

Aleks laughed but then went silent when spotting the glare Angela threw him. Aleks cleared his throat to get everyone's attention. "We all need to stick together. I know we all want to rip Starburn's head off, but doing so will kill Kyra. And we don't want that. We all need to pitch in and help find a loophole to this bond."

Someone must've filled Aleks in about our situation, and my heart jumped from his words. The guy was only here for a day, and he was ready to get into action.

Siddiqis was glaring at Aleks. "Look who grew a brain."

Aleks glared at Siddiqis as well. "I also grew muscles, so one knock to the face and you'll be out like a light."

Siddiqis chuckled. Darkly. "You know what happens the second you hurt me."

Aleks glanced at me and then went back to glaring at Siddiqis, who was grinning like the devil he was. "Just you wait until we get that bond broken. Then you're in for it." He had a murderous look in his eyes.

Siddiqis raised an eyebrow. "You don't stand a chance against a hybrid, Silvermoon. Remember that."

Aleks fumed there, and I realized I had to put an end to this before it got out of hand. "You two, stop. We need to focus on the future. We need to work together to break the bond."

Siddiqis shrugged. "Whatever." He said it with his "I don't care" voice that pissed everyone off, especially Aleks.

Something silver flashed and then hit Siddiqis in the shoulder. A knife. Before I could do anything, I felt a searing pain in my right shoulder, in the exact spot where Siddiqis was hit. I cried out in pain and surprise as blood poured out of the wound.

Gustav was on my side in an instant, gathering napkins to stop the blood flow. Siddiqis sat there, also shocked and in pain as I was. Angela was running to get more napkins and a doctor, while Boota and Darq ran to my side. Stefan just froze, unsure about what to do as Laylita ran over to me with a horrified look. Everyone was shocked and horrified.

Aleks, his hand still out, looked the most horrified as realization struck him that he had hurt me badly. He ran to me and grabbed my left hand with both of his, looking as if he were about to cry. "I'm so sorry, Kyra. I wasn't thinking. I'm sorry. Oh god. I'm so–"

"It's all right, Aleks. I know. It's all right," I interrupted. "Nice throw by the way. Save it for when we get this bond broken." I heard the dining room door close, and we all looked up. After a minute, I realized who left. "Where the hell did Siddiqis go?" I moaned.

Gustav shook his head. "He's wounded. He can't go much farther before the loss of blood gets to him." He turned to Stefan, who was now on his feet. "Stefan, follow me. We have a hybrid to catch."

Stefan nodded, and the two of them left the dining hall. Aleks kept apologizing over and over again, while Boota held my right hand as Darq ran to tell Angela to hurry up. Angela still wasn't back with the damn doctor, and I was losing blood fast. Aleks finally stopped apologizing and started to inspect the wound. It was a deep stab but wasn't anywhere near my heart, so chances were I was going to live.

I winced at the pain. "Well, this breakfast just went swell." A little voice in the back of my head piped in, saying, *Why isn't the wound healing?* but I shushed that voice away.

Aleks shushed me. "The more you speak, the more it'll hurt. Just breathe." He was pale with shock, but his eyes were full of the urge to help me.

Boota had streaks of tears running down her face, and her shoulders were shaking hard. "Boota, don't cry. I'll be okay. You'll upset the baby." I urged her.

She nodded, now hiccupping vigorously. Aleks let go of my hand to give Boota a glass of water. She drank all of it, and the hiccups stopped.

Finally, Angela and Darq came running in to the dining hall with the castle doctor in tow. "It took forever, but we found him!"

Angela said through ragged breathing, showing that she clearly was running at full speed.

The doctor hurried to me and motioned for Aleks to carry me. "I need to take her to the castle infirmary. There, she can lie down, and I can help stop the bleeding."

Aleks swooped me into his arms, muscles flexing at work. He wasn't joking about the muscles. I felt lightheaded. The loss of blood was getting to me, and the last thing I heard before I fainted was "Crap!"

# CHAPTER 12

## The Infirmary

WHEN I CAME back to my senses, I was lying on a bed, feeling like crap. I tried to get up, but I fell back down on my back with a groan the second I felt a blasting pain shoot through me. I reached to touch my injured bare right shoulder and felt smooth skin. My skin had healed up, but it was still sore. I realized I was wearing a tank top and sweat pants instead of the tank top or jeans I was wearing at breakfast.

Suddenly, I remembered what had happened at dinner and started to get up again, only to be stopped by a familiar voice. "I suggest you keep lying down."

I looked to my right to see Siddiqis on the bed beside me, staring at me with his cool magenta eyes. I shivered. "I don't have to listen to you."

He smirked. "No, you don't. But if you're smart, you will listen to me."

I ignored him and instantly regretted it; I felt vomit rise up to my throat, and I leaned over the side to puke directly into the garbage can. I coughed and then wiped my mouth with the napkin placed beside the bed and drank all the water in the cup beside me. I settled back and huffed. "What are you doing here?"

He also settled back against the bed and sighed. "The bond. I get hurt, you get hurt."

"Yeah, I know about the bond. I mean, what are you doing here? You ran off when you got hit, and now you're here."

He ran his left hand through his hair. "My shoulder's still sore. Plus I woke up here. I'm assuming I fell unconscious, because all I remember was running and then falling and blacking out. When I woke up, I found myself here, and you were still unconscious."

I frowned at the ceiling. "Why did you run off? That was a stupid move, considering running with an open wound meant faster blood loss."

He sighed again. "I don't know. Something just told me to run. I wasn't even thinking. I just took off, running as fast as I could, but it was hard with the whole injured shoulder." I heard him turn in his bed, and I knew he was now looking at me. "Don't you wonder why we didn't heal faster?"

I gave that a thought. I never actually gave it a lot of thought about why I didn't heal as fast as I should have had. "I have no clue. That's strange."

"Very. You don't think that this bond took away some of our powers, do you? Like our ability to heal?" I heard slight panic in his tone.

"No, I don't think so. I mean, I still feel the same. Do you?"

"I feel the same too. But still, they never said that this could happen. At the academy, they didn't mention this in prophecy study."

I turned in my bed, wincing at the pain, and stared back into Siddiqis's eyes. "Let's be honest. The academy barely taught us anything except for 'All things come with a price' and 'Don't get hobgoblins mad.'"

Siddiqis chuckled. "You forgot, 'If the vampire wants a latte, the vampire wants a latte.'"

I laughed, and he laughed as well, and it was like we were fourteen years old again, sitting on our beds, looking at each other, and laughing at some joke he would make. It felt good and weird. It felt like the good old times.

Then the moment was gone the second the infirmary doors opened, and in came my husband. Siddiqis and I stopped laughing to look up and meet Gustav's shocked stare. He pointed at me, then to Siddiqis, back to me, back to Siddiqis, and then gestured between us.

Siddiqis and I just stared back at him, unable to tell what he was trying to say.

He threw his hands in the air and then stormed out, slamming the doors shut.

We were silent. Then Siddiqis spoke. "That was unexpected."

"You took the words right out of my mouth," I replied.

Silence. And then, "Don't you find it weird that we couldn't hear him come? Like, what's with our hearing?"

I nodded. "That is weird. First our healing, and now our hearing? What next?"

He shook his head. "I have no clue, but it probably won't be good."

*****

Siddiqis and I started to talk about old memories, and after fifteen minutes, we were laughing so hard we both fell off our beds and landed on the floor beside each other, facing the ceiling.

We were chuckling when the doors of the infirmary flew open, and both of us jumped to our feet to meet Angela's shocked stare.

She came in and raised an eyebrow. "It sounded like some funny reality show was on, but it's just you two. So is there something I'm missing?" She added after seeing our confused expressions, "You know, since you two were on the floor, laughing like good friends?"

I cleared my throat. "We were just talking about old times. That's all. Right, Siddiqis?" I looked at him.

He also cleared his voice and then spoke. "Yeah, what she said. Nothing that will appeal to your sense of humor."

Angela sighed. "C'mon. Can't you show some feelings? I get that you died and you've been dead for a while now, but if Kyra can show some emotion, then you can too." She stood with her hands on her hips, her signature stance.

He stared at her. "Like Kyra said, we were only talking."

Angela eyed him and then shrugged. Then she turned to me. "Can we go for a walk? I need to talk to you." She looked at Siddiqis and back to me, her gaze steady. "Alone."

I looked at her with a questioning look. Angela wasn't one to ask to go on a walk; she was the type of person that killed demons if she had a bad hair day. "Okay. Sure." I looked at Siddiqis, who just stared at the ground, and left the room with Angela by my side.

We walked down the hallway and made a turn. I stopped at the top of the stairs and looked at her. She looked at me, questioning. "What are you going to do?" she asked.

I smiled, an idea popping into my head as well as the sense of déjà vu. "I wonder if I'm rusty."

She stared at me, and then realization struck her about what I was thinking about doing. "Oh my god. Not again. Kyra, don't you dare—"

I didn't wait to hear the end of her complaint. I leapt over the railing, feeling the falling sensation for a second, and heard a scream, and then I landed on my feet, on the floor. I definitely wasn't rusty.

I turned around and looked up to Angela's shocked expression. Her mouth was open, and I realized that she was the one who screamed. She looked down at me with shock and true amazement. "You got hit by a knife in the frigging shoulder, and yet you are still able to jump from one floor down to another. You amaze me, girl."

I smiled. "I'm the Chosen Hybrid. I live by the terms of awesome and amazement."

She pointed a finger down at me. "Hey, don't push it. You only get one good comment from me a day."

I laughed, and she laughed too. Then she ran down the stairs and motioned to the front door. I pulled it open, and both of us went out the door, into the fresh morning air. Wait. Morning? I looked at Angela, confused. "How is it still morning? How long was I out? An hour?"

Angela eyed me cautiously. "Honey, it's not Friday anymore." She sighed at my questioning expression. "It's Wednesday."

My eyes widened with shock as I took it all in. "I've been unconscious for five days?" I whispered.

"Yep. For six days you were in some coma, except you would come in and out, and you would try to kill anyone who was at arm's length. Did you know we had to tie you down to the bed on Sunday because you had punched Darq in the face? He has a huge bruise and–" She saw my expression. "Kyra, you were totally out of it. You couldn't have known what was happening."

I shook my head. "You're wrong."

"What do you mean?"

"I wasn't in a coma, Angela."

"What?"

"I was having this nightmare. For six whole days, I've been having this horrible nightmare that was so lifelike. It was as if the nightmare had gone on forever, and every time a figure would attack me, I'd fight back. When I was strangling the person trying to hurt me, it felt real. Everything felt real."

She sighed. "Well, I can explain the strangling part, because you tried strangling me." When I looked back at her, she pulled aside her hair, and there they were. Finger marks. I had strangled her, and very hard at that.

I gasped. "I'm so sorry." I couldn't say anything else. I was in shock. Shame reddened my face.

Angela sighed. "It's okay. You were suffering from a nightmare."

I shook my head. "I should've been more careful. I should've known it was a nightmare–"

"Kyra. It's okay. I'm okay. Don't worry, I'm fine." She smiled, but I saw it was slightly forced.

I nodded, but I wasn't buying it. I was not done talking about this. We began walking down the path toward the town. We walked in silence. Finally, I spoke. "So what's wrong?"

She looked at me suddenly. "Huh?"

"You said you wanted to walk with me. That's probably your way of saying you want to talk about something that's on your mind." She looked nervous. "Angela Scarblood, what's wrong?"

Angela pressed her lips together. "I'm in a pickle."

"What's up?"

"Well, everyone's found love. You and Gustav, Boota and Darq, Bonzai and what's-her-face."

"Nebula. Nebula Du Flare, a powerful fire faerie, I believe."

"Yeah, her. The point is, everyone's either married or in love, and I'm just the third wheel."

I softened up. "Angela, you will never be a third wheel. And as for your love life, you will find someone."

"Kyra, I think I'm in love, but I don't know."

"Who's the lucky guy?"

She sighed happily in thought, something she never did a lot. "His name is Luke Hathfire. He's a fire warlock. He's got a dreamy lean body, with scars his boss gave him after he didn't make a delivery. Oh, he works in the Bat Cave with Aleks, though the two don't talk. He's got this golden tan and this cute British accent because he, like, traveled and stayed in Britain a lot, and he's got these green eyes that just–"

"Whoa, alert the media! Angela Scarblood has a case of the love fever!" I laughed. Angela wasn't one to fall for someone.

She laughed. "I know. It's crazy, right?"

"Yes, very crazy indeed. But I'm glad that you are in . . ." I paused, stopping dead in my tracks. "What did you say the guy's name was?"

She looked taken back. "Luke Hathfire."

My stomach dropped. I knew that name. I knew it too well. My only question was, From where though? I turned quickly on the ball of my foot and took off running back to the castle, full vampire speed. I heard Angela running behind me, shouting for me to slow down, but I didn't wait for her. I threw open the front doors and ran to Gustav's and my room. I kicked it open and stopped in the middle of the room, closing the door behind me. "Gustav!" I shouted.

I heard the shower door open and saw the bathroom door open with a bang. Then out came Gustav, wearing only a towel at his waist, his hair wet and glistening. He looked at me, panicked. "What's wrong? Are you hurt? What happened? You look flustered." He strode to me and held a hand to my cheek. He smelled like mint, bringing back the times before we were married.

I grabbed his other hand with both of mine. "Gustav, do you know anyone named Luke Hathfire?"

He thought about it and slowly nodded. "I've heard the name. I'm not sure from where though."

"He's supposedly a bartender like Aleks in the Bat Cave, but, Gustav, I know that name from somewhere bad."

"Relax, love. Do you remember where you've heard his name from?"

I looked up into his blue eyes. "No. But I know he's bad news. I feel it. I've heard that name before."

He sighed. "You know we can't arrest him without proof that he's a bad guy. I'll tell you what. I'll look deeper into this guy's past and see what I can do. In the meantime, you should be resting."

I shook my head. "I'm okay. I can walk, talk, I literally ran here and kicked open the door."

"Well then, I guess you're all right, but at it slow please."

"Yeah." Then a thought occurred to me. "Gustav, what happened early today? In the infirmary?"

He was silent. And then he spoke. "I came in, and when I saw you and Siddiqis together, I felt somewhat jealous." He looked down.

I softened. "Gustav, you are my husband. I'm yours, always and forever."

He smiled and then lowered his lips onto mine. We embraced each other in the kiss, a hot urge passing between us as the kiss brought us together and more alive. It was intensifying, the heat of the kiss. It was very pleasurable, soothing me of all my worries. My only thoughts were of Gustav and how everything was going to be okay soon.

Of course, the moment broke when Angela appeared in our doorway, looking flustered and out of breath. "You . . . have got . . . to stop . . . running . . . so damn . . . fast." Then she saw us looking flustered and cloudy and realized what she interrupted. "Oh. My bad. I'm going to, um, go now. See you guys at dinner, since lunch is canceled." She waved and then turned on her heel and walked away. Her footsteps echoed in the hall, going farther and farther away from us.

I looked up at Gustav. "Why is it that every time I kiss anyone, someone always comes crashing through the door? A little ironic, don't you think?"

He chuckled. "That's true. We need stronger doors."

"Ha." Then I paused. "Wait. Why's lunch canceled?"

He sighed. "After the whole knife thing, everyone has been just doing their own thing. You and Siddiqis were stuck in the infirmary. Boota has been in bed with Darq, never leaving her side, and same goes for Laylita. Aleks has just been wandering the hallways like a ghost, and Stefan isn't coming out of his rooms." He shook his head. "Everyone's in lockdown mode."

I sighed. "Well, we still have to find a way to break the bond, and we need all the help we can get."

Gustav nodded and then smiled. "Does that mean I can go round up all our friends for a meeting?" He had a twinkle in his eyes, and I knew he was tired of not having a lot of action as we did last year.

I smiled. "Yes. Go get our friends and call the representatives of every clan in Xercus, Servic, and the Mortal Portal. It's time to get down to business."

# CHAPTER 13

## The Meeting

"THIS IS INSANE!" I turned my gaze over to Mr. Darkwoods, who was glaring at me, while rubbing my forehead. "What is insane, Darkwoods?"

He turned a fuming red. "Last year, you said all our problems were solved. And that Siddiqis Starburn would be dead for eternity, yet here he is, standing before us with no guards to make sure he doesn't kill one of us."

Gustav stepped in, his voice deep. "I understand the confusion of Siddiqis being here, but let me assure you that he isn't posing a threat at the moment, and so he is the least of my concerns. We have bigger matters, such as my wife being bonded to him."

It was like this for two hours in the meeting hall. After ten minutes of calling all allied leaders, we had a few more than a dozen representatives from Xercus, Servic, and the Mortal Portal, as well as Mr. Darkwoods. We decided not to call in Aries just yet, considering he would have freaked. So we thought we could handle a few reps. It was apparent ten minutes later that it wasn't a walk in the park when one vamp leader from Servic made an attempt to kill Siddiqis.

Siddiqis was pacing, glaring at the vamp that almost sank her fangs into him. She shrank back into her seat. Siddiqis cleared his throat. "Gustav is right. We need to break this bond."

"And how do you suppose we do that?" The representative of the werewolf pack in Xercus hissed.

Aleks piped in from his seat. "We could ask the Book of Prophecies again?"

Angela seated next to me shook her head. "The book said that Death will break the bond."

Mr. Darkwoods got to his feet. "So we kill Siddiqis. Easy as that, right?"

Siddiqis scowled. "Wrong. Kill me, you kill her." He jabbed a thumb toward me.

Mr. Darkwoods seemed unfazed.

Gustav growled. "We are not killing my wife."

Mr. Darkwoods held up his hands in both defeat and annoyance.

Gustav sighed. "We all need to find a way to break the bond, but the problem is, how do we break it without killing Rumblen?"

"And Siddiqis," Siddiqis piped in.

"Yeah, whatever," Gustav muttered, earning a glare from Siddiqis.

I cleared my throat. "Should we make a visit to the library? Collect all the information we can on how to find prophecy loopholes?"

Gustav leaned back in his chair. "You are not going anywhere near the library."

"Why?"

"Because the last time you went to that library, you came out dead. I'm not taking that risk."

I looked at Siddiqis and saw he was looking at me. I knew exactly by his facial expression what he was thinking about. I looked away, back at Gustav. "I don't think I'm in any danger. Plus I can take anyone on."

Gustav gave me the famous "don't argue with me on this" look, and I decided to back down. I wasn't feeling well anyways.

Aleks sighed. "I'll go to the library. But I'll need some people to go with me."

"I'll come," Angela said, jumping to her feet.

Gustav smiled. "Finally, we make some progress. Okay, you two, head straight to the library." He pointed at Aleks. "Be armed, just in case. Angela can take care of herself. You, not so much."

Aleks scowled but nodded grumpily. He and Angela went, and it was just the representatives, Mr. Darkwoods, Siddiqis, Gustav, and I.

Mr. Darkwoods cleared his voice. "How can I help?"

Gustav looked at him. "If you and the other leaders can keep a close eye out for any useful information, that will be appreciated. Representatives, please report back to your pack leaders what has been discussed in today's meeting."

All the representatives and Mr. Darkwoods nodded and took their leave. Then it was just Siddiqis, Gustav, and I.

Siddiqis sighed and fell into a chair. "What do I do?"

Gustav responded without hesitation. "Nothing. Just stay in the castle, and we'll take care of it."

"Fine by me."

I piped in. "What about me?"

Gustav pointed at me. "You can stay in the castle, like Siddiqis."

"Or?" I asked.

He laughed without humor. "Yeah, no. You don't get another option. You need to stay here. Boota and Laylita need you. I plan on sending Darq and Stefan on a boys' night out."

I raised an eyebrow. "I'm linked to my ex-boyfriend, who is also the guy that killed me before, and you want to send our two becoming fathers on a boys' night out?"

Gustav chuckled. "Fine. No boys' night out. I'll just tell both of them to stay with their wives."

I nodded. "Good. Also, keep an eye on Stefan. He needs to support Laylita, and if he has any plans on killing her, we convict him of treason."

Gustav nodded. "Fine with me. All right, I'm going to go finish the shower I was having two and a half hours ago. See you guys." He gave me a peck on the cheek, nodded at Siddiqis, and left the room, his footsteps echoing.

Siddiqis and I were silent. Then I spoke. "Well, what do we do? We're on house arrest."

Siddiqis gave it a thought. Then he snapped his fingers. "We should go to the castle library. There's got to be something there, right?"

I nodded. "Nice. Let's do it then."

We both walked through the door, down the hall. We walked across the foyer and past the training room. Siddiqis smiled as we passed the room, and I couldn't help but be curious. "Why are you smiling?"

He looked at me. "I was just remembering those times we used to train together. You were so determined to knock me off my feet you would say something was behind me, and when I looked back, you'd knock me down. And you always did that, and I always knew there was nothing behind me, but I still always looked."

I peered at him, now lost in the memory and lost in the way he talked about our past so preciously like it was a pearl. I smiled. "I didn't know you knew there was nothing behind you."

He chuckled. "You did that every day. It was obvious after the third time you knocked me down. I just looked behind because you enjoyed getting to knock me over."

I grinned. "Yeah. It was fun."

"Yeah."

Silence was exchanged as we walked down the hallway. I sighed. "What if we don't break this bond?"

"We will. There's always a loophole."

I nodded, and we finally made it to the castle library. I threw open the doors, and the both of us stepped inside, the door shutting behind us.

The library was my favorite place in the castle, besides my bedroom and the training room. The walls were lined with books, and there was an area for reading next to the window, where I usually stayed. In the middle of the room were a desk and a computer.

I strode into the room and stood in front of the shelves. "You check what you can find online. I'll search the books," I told Siddiqis without turning to look at him.

"Okay," he said, and I heard him move across the hardwood floor and take a seat in the chair, and he started the computer up.

I looked through several sections, searching for anything that looked ancient and promising an explanation. I found books on ancient Xercus history, the geography of all the countries, maps from the Old Times, novels, and more boring geography books.

After a two-hour search, I was still empty-handed. I looked over my shoulder to Siddiqis, who was staring at the computer in frustration. "Any luck?"

He looked up at me and sighed. "Nothing. There is absolutely nothing helpful to breaking the bond."

"I still have one more shelf—"

"Kyra, it's useless. We can't break the bond without dying. This search was just pointless!" He slammed a fist down next to the keyboard, splintering the wooden desk.

I groaned. "That was mahogany. Aries loved that desk."

He sighed. "Sorry."

"It's fine. There's got to be a way, Siddiqis."

"And I'd love nothing else but to find that way. Unfortunately, it seems that there is no other way, Kyra."

"You said there's always a loophole!" I nearly yelled, impatience and rage bubbling inside of me.

"Yeah, but apparently, I'm wrong about a lot of things!" he yelled back, clearly also pissed.

"What's that suppose to mean?"

"It means, I was wrong that you still loved me!"

I felt like a bucket of ice-cold water was dumped on my head. His last words rang in my ears, as shock completely paralyzed me. I couldn't speak; I was that stunned.

Siddiqis was also stunned by what he just said, and I guessed he didn't mean for that to slip out. We just stared at each other in stunned silence and shock, waiting to recover.

Siddiqis recovered first, though his voice shook a little. "I'm sorry. That just slipped out."

I cleared my throat, still shaken up. "Why would you think that I still love you?"

He looked at me with saddened eyes. "There was little hope I had. And now that hope disappeared into thin air."

"Siddiqis—"

The library doors suddenly banged open, and in came Darq, running toward us, eyes frantic.

I jumped at the sound of the door banging open. "Darq, what's wrong?"

He was panting. "The baby . . ."

I felt fear creep into my heart. "What's wrong with the baby? Is Boota all right?"

Darq shook his head. "The baby. He's coming." He looked up at Siddiqis and my stunned face. "He's coming right now."

# CHAPTER 14

## Another Deatheye

DARQ AND I ran out of the library to Boota's room, while Siddiqis stayed behind, looking for more about the prophecy. We ran up the steps and turned the corner to Aries's room, where Boota was. When we approached the door, all we could hear were Boota's screams of pain. I broke into the room even though the door wasn't locked, with Darq following in behind me.

Boota's wails made it seem like there was a crowd of people. But in reality, there were only six people: Boota, the castle doctor, a nurse, Angela, Aleks, and Gustav. Upon our arrival, everyone except Boota turned to look at us.

Gustav came to me and engulfed me in a hug. I hugged him tightly, and when I let go, I gazed at Boota, who was in a white nightgown and was in terrible pain. "How's she been?" I asked Gustav.

He shook his head. "Not good. It's been forty-six minutes, and she's really tired. I'm not sure she'll be able to push the baby out."

Fear climbed up to my heart. "This baby is not going to die." I turned to the doctor, who was looking a little worried. "What's the status on the baby's arrival?"

"The baby appears to be ready to come. Mrs. Deatheye's water has broken, and she's in labor. But it seems that Mrs. Deatheye is too weak to push out the child." He shook his head. "I'm afraid the child may die."

Upon hearing this, Boota let out a heartbreaking wail. I went to her and held her hand. "Hey, don't worry. Fight the pain, Boota. This baby is counting on you. Just push."

Boota, sweating heavily, grunted and pushed, groaning and screaming each time. She kept pushing and pushing, and as she pushed harder, her screams grew into a strange animal sound. She clearly was in so much pain.

Suddenly, we heard a thump. I whirled around to see the doctor on the ground, unconscious. My heart dropped. You've got to be kidding me, I thought in disbelief. Everyone was silent with shock, except for Boota, who kept pushing.

Gustav knelt to the doctor's side and checked his pulse. He looked up. "He's still alive," he said in disbelief. "He fainted."

I gawked. "What kind of a doctor faints in the middle of childbirth?"

"Apparently, the ones who aren't very good at being doctors," Aleks muttered loud enough for me to hear.

Darq shook his head. "Oh god. Who's going to deliver the baby?" There was panic on his face and in his voice.

Angela looked prepared to throw up. "We need to deliver the baby. Now."

As everyone argued, I stared at Boota. My friend was sweating and was red with exhaustion. She was screaming in pain, and the nurse beside her looked confused and panicked. The poor woman was never told what to do when the doctor fainted.

An idea came to me. I addressed my friends, still looking at Boota. "I'll do it."

Everyone stopped talking to stare at me with disbelief. Gustav spoke. "Rumblen, dear, you don't know how to deliver a baby."

"I've seen a show or two. It's our only chance."

He looked like he was going to say no again, but then Darq started to talk. "Do it. You're right. It's our only chance at this point."

I nodded, feeling a loadful of pressure on my shoulders. I took in a breath and breathe out slowly. Then I turned to my friends and the nurse, who looked at me with awe. "Nurse, I need a bowl of warm water, a towel, scissors, and a lighter. Darq, come hold Boota's hand. Gustav and Aleks, wait outside. Angela, stay in here and lock the door behind the guys."

Both guys looked ready to protest, but when Boota let out a wail, both of them walked right out of the room and Angela locked it when they left. The nurse went through the cart of tools she had brought in before and set everything I needed on the coffee table. Aries is not going to be thrilled about me delivering a baby in his room, I thought, pulling on a pair of surgeon gloves, and I mentally pulled my big girl pants on.

I motioned for Darq to go to Boota, and without hesitating, he took her hand in his. I walked over to the foot of the bed and took in a deep breath. Then I went under the sheets. From under the sheets, I saw the top of the baby's head. "I see the head!"

"Push, Boota, push!" Angela urged Boota, who was clinging to Angela now as well, resulting a scream of pain as she pushed. The baby's head came out and then its shoulders. Boota was panting harder, and I feared, with her breathing like this, she was going to pass out. So, I grabbed the baby's head and gently pulled it out of my friend. The baby slid out into my arms. I called from under the sheet. "I need scissors and a lighter." A second later, I had scissors, and carefully I cut the umbilical cord and burned the ends of it.

I came out from under the covers, with Boota and Darq's newborn child in my arms. I looked up at Darq and Boota, who were both staring at me, expectantly. "You've got a beautiful baby boy." They lit up with joy and Darq started kissing a crying Boota. "I need a towel," I told the nurse.

The nurse rushed over to me with a towel and stared in awe as I wrapped its body. Then, ever so slightly, I patted the child's back to get it breathing. But he wouldn't breathe. I felt a pang of worry go through me. I listened for a heartbeat. There wasn't any coming from the newborn boy.

No, I thought, patting the child's back a little harder. This couldn't be happening. I shook the child a little. "Hey, little guy. Come on, breathe."

No response.

I dipped my fingers into his mouth to remove any fluid, but it didn't help. The newborn wasn't breathing. I patted it harder. "C'mon. Don't die. No, don't die." I moaned. I felt hot tears slipping down my face onto the child. I looked up at Angela, who was now staring at me with a horrified look. "He's not breathing."

Boota and Darq looked at me, suddenly aware that the child wasn't crying. Boota started to cry, Darq holding her while crying silently. It was horrible.

I looked down at the child, thinking. When I came out, I wasn't breathing. But the child isn't a hybrid. What can it be? I wondered, staring at the child's silent face. He was beautiful, with a striking complexion. There was something peculiar about the vibe I got from him. Then I realized what was wrong. It didn't seem possible, but it was.

I looked up to Angela. "Call in Gustav."

She looked at me strangely but still opened the bedroom door and called Gustav in. My husband waltzed in, and when he saw the scene, he stopped. When he saw me holding the silent child, he came to me with a stunned look in his eyes. "It can't be."

I looked up at him. "Gustav, I don't think the child's dead."

"What? Rumblen, he's not breathing."

"Yeah, but I came out not breathing."

"There's no way he's a hybrid."

"No, he isn't. But what about a dark angel?"

Gustav looked glassy eyed as he gave it a thought. Then he gave me a confused look. "How can he be a dark angel? He would need to be cursed."

I looked at Boota and Darq. "Are there any death angels that have something against you?"

Boota shook her head, but Darq remained silent.

Uh-oh. "Darq, what did you do to get a death angel angry?" I demanded.

He looked at Boota and then sighed. "I may have had an encounter with a death angel at a bar before Boota and I got married, and I may have had said something stupid and got him angry. I was wasted, okay! To be fair, I had a horrible hangover."

I breathed out. "If I weren't relieved, I would kill you right now. That means the child still has a chance."

Gustav frowned. "But, Rumblen, dark angels come out and open their eyes. This one isn't opening his eyes."

I tried feeling the newborns emotions, but it wasn't expressing any emotion. It was like a brick wall; I was getting nothing out of it. The child must have been cursed with no emotions.

I looked up at Boota and Darq again with an idea. "Would you like to hold him?"

They looked at each other and then at me. "Yes," both of them answered at the same time.

I walked over to the bed and laid the child in Boota's arms. She looked down at him and smiled, tears in her eyes. "Dark angel or not, I still love him."

I smiled. "What's his name?"

Gustav smiled to himself, knowing what I was trying to do.

Boota looked up at Darq, but he shook his head. "It's your call. Anything you pick I will love." He was smiling down at the child with a beautiful glow in his face.

Boota looked down at the child and leaned closer to him and whispered in his ear, "Prince Mason Deatheye."

The child's eyes opened. We all gasped in amazement as Boota looked into the child's eyes with complete and utter shock. He had cold gray eyes, the same color as Darq's but colder. He was a beauty but scary at the same time.

I sighed in relief. "Dark angels awaken when hearing their name. You've given birth to a dark angel, who is cursed with no emotions."

Boota looked worried at that. "No emotions? Will he be ruthless?"

I considered it. "Possibly. But we will make sure he grows up to use his curse as an advantage. I have no idea how we can break the curse, so we're going to have to live with it."

Darq was busy studying his child, stroking his face with his finger. The child grabbed his finger, and Darq looked swoony. "I've already fell in love with our child. Our little boy."

Suddenly, the door banged open, and in came Aleks, with Laylita clutching his arm for balance and Stefan, who looked like he was forced to come. He must have been.

Aleks looked at the scene in front of him and smiled. "Where's the new Deatheye?"

Boota smiled as well. "Over here."

He went over to her side, let Laylita sit on the edge of the bed, and looked down at the newborn. "What's his name?"

"Mason Deatheye."

"Can I hold him?"

"Sure," Boota replied happily, and she carefully handed Aleks her new child.

Aleks carefully took Mason into his arms and peered down at it with pure curiosity and love. Mason studied him with his big gray eyes, now less coldly. Aleks laughed. "A dark angel. He will definitely be adored. I mean, look how big his eyes are!" He really loved Mason. Aleks wasn't used to babies, so when he saw one, he turned into gushy mode.

We all watched Aleks make goo-goo sounds at Mason while the baby was just staring up at him with a studying expression. We all chuckled as the baby sneezed, and Aleks went into mushy mode, commenting on the child's skin, on his eyes, and on his expression.

Laylita sat on the edge of the bed, staring at Aleks with a longing expression. Stefan was just uncomfortable. I knew Stefan would choose to leave Laylita once the child was born. I pushed the thought out of my head though.

A knock came from the door, and I told everyone I'd get it. I walked to the door and opened it.

Siddiqis stood there with his hands on his knees, bent over and panting. He looked up, and I knew why he had run.

I looked back to see everyone staring at me. "Excuse me for a second. I'll be back soon."

They all nodded, and I shut the door behind me. Siddiqis and I walked down the hallway as I held him up because he was too tired to walk on his own. "You okay?" I asked.

He shook his head. "My speed is gone too. The bond is slowing our powers down. But that's not important right now." He stopped and looked me in the eye, a flare in his magenta eyes. "I found something."

Excitement bubbled inside of me. "What did you find?"

"Oh nothing . . ." He grinned. "Except for a way to break this bond!"

I squealed with happiness. "Oh my god! This is great news!" I threw my arms around him, and we hugged. It wasn't after five seconds that I realized whom I was hugging. I let him go and looked away, a little embarrassed by my sudden reaction.

Siddiqis looked glassy eyed, but then he recovered. "So you coming or what?"

I cleared my throat. "Yeah."

We walked down the hallway in awkward silence, and when we were standing in front of the library doors, Siddiqis pushed them open for me, and I walked in with him behind me.

I walked over to the table, splintered from when Siddiqis raged at it. "All right. Show me the way to breaking the bond."

Siddiqis walked past me and to the last shelf I didn't check. "When you left, I started looking at every book on this shelf. When I thought that I had searched every book, I saw that there was one book that both of us didn't look at." He searched the spines and pulled out a humongous book.

I gawked. "That's as big as the Book of Prophecies! How did we not see that?"

"We find the things we need in the most obvious places, thinking it would never be there."

"Well, what does the book say?"

He blew the top of the cover, coughing at all the dust. "It's a book full of history behind the prophecies and how the prophecies were made. Something MP Academy never had in prophecy study."

"Have you read it?"

"Nope. I was waiting to read it with you."

I walked over to him and waited for him to open the book. When it became apparent he wasn't, I cleared my throat. "Any day now."

He sighed. "Yeah. The other reason I didn't read the book is because the damn thing won't open. It's sealed shut." He tried opening it, but it wouldn't budge.

"Here, let me try."

He passed the book to me, a look of hope on his face. I studied the cover of the book. The title was The History behind the Prophecies. It was a big leather book, and when I tried to open it, it was like someone had glued it shut.

I sighed. "We found a book that can help us. But we can't open it."

Siddiqis looked at me, and by the glint in his eyes, I knew he had an idea. "Let's do what we did to bring the Book of Prophecies."

I nodded, and then we balanced the book on both of our arms as we gripped each other's forearms. We looked at each other. "Open," we commanded in unison.

Suddenly, the book's cover flew open. Siddiqis grinned. "Are you ready?" he asked me.

I looked at him and smiled. "I'm ready."

# CHAPTER 15

## When Riddles Are Revealed

WE SET THE book down on the table and sat side by side, reading the book. It was full of information on how the prophecies were created.

Siddiqis read it out loud. "'Over a thousand years ago, there was a time when there was no such thing as the prophecy. That was a time when anything could happen, and nothing was predictable. Then the Prophecy Sisters were born—two different souls bound to be together. They were as powerful as angels and as dangerous as demons. They were the first hybrids. Their parents were both good and bad, balancing each other out. As the sisters grew older, they realized that they had a gift. They were able to see into the future, and so began their reign of glory. They predicted storms, troubles, and anything they saw.

"'But one day, one of the sisters lost her sight. She couldn't see anything. Many say that it's her grief of not being able to see that caused prophecies to become bad. She became known as Death, the dark sister who spoke of horrible prophecies. The other sister became known as Karma, the light sister who spoke of great and successful prophecies. Though both sisters were so different, they always kept the other company. The world loved them and wrote stories about the great and powerful Prophecy Sisters.

"'Until one day, the sisters vanished. They were gone without a trace. They just disappeared. That is when Heaven created the great Book of Prophecies. It's said that every time a prophecy is fulfilled, the sisters would secretly contact Heaven and write in the Book of Prophecies about what they see or sense. Then when someone wants to know the prophecy, the Book of Prophecies became the go-to book.

"'But no one has ever seen the sisters. Legend has it that the sisters fled to somewhere far away, in uncharted lands. They can only be summoned by two hybrids. Though many have tried, they have not been able to find the Prophecy Sisters. Many believe that the sisters would strike down anyone other than hybrids that tried to summon them, so no one had tried to in fear for their life.'"

Siddiqis sighed. "This is long but better than prophecy study."

I nodded. "So the prophecies are created by the Prophecy Sisters, who then send the Book of Prophecies to Heaven for the angels to see." I groaned. "But it still doesn't say how we break the bond."

Siddiqis nodded. "It only talks about the sisters, and it says that they have never been seen."

I thought about it, and then it hit me. "Siddiqis, what are the sisters' names?"

He looked down at the page, searching for the names. When he found it, he pointed at the names. "Death, the dark sister, and Karma, the light sister."

I shook my head in stunned amazement. "That's it."

He looked up at me. "What?"

"Siddiqis, the prophecy said, 'The Sinner must take his place beside the Chosen Hybrid, for both are a whole.'" He still didn't understand, so I went on, "'To fulfill the Sinner and the Chosen Hybrid prophecy, the connection must be broken by the hands of Death. Then Karma will fulfill the deed.'"

He looked at me, realization hitting him. "Are you saying—"

"Althaea read it wrong. It doesn't mean death and karma will break the bond—"

"It's the sisters, Death and Karma, that will," he finished my sentence and grinned at me. "You're a genius."

"Siddiqis, we can't just summon the Prophecy Sisters. Did you not just hear what you read about the sisters striking down whoever summoned them?"

"It says 'anyone other than hybrids.' We are hybrids. We need to at least try summoning them." He groaned at my hesitant look. "C'mon, Kyra! We need to. It's the only way."

"How do we even summon them?"

He looked back at the book and read from where we stopped. "'In order to contact the Prophecy Sisters, two hybrids, and only two hybrids, must travel to the Cursed Caves, where it's said that the Prophecy Sisters can be contacted.'"

"Cursed Caves? Why is it that everything must be cursed or forbidden or great?"

He shrugged. "How am I supposed to know? I'm reading the book with you, and I just learned that two twins with psychic powers make the prophecies."

I walked over to the shelves of maps, pulled out the most recently made, and unrolled it on the table, over the book. It opened up, and the map was freshly labeled. We both leaned on our elbows to look at the map, like children observing a book together.

I pointed at the Cursed Caves on the map. "The Cursed Caves are in the Maledicta Terra. We will have to go through Servic, Jesarala, and Possull! That will take more than a week by foot."

"But we can't go through Jesarala and Possull since they aren't the friendliest country, so we'll have to go around the countries, so we will be travelling along the perimeter of Jesarala and Possull, but we will be in the Maledicta Terra for a long time."

I dropped my voice low. "Siddiqis, the Maledicta Terra is Latin for 'cursed is the land.' We will not make it."

"It's our only shot, Kyra."

He was right. I licked my lips. "All right. We will leave this Friday. I need to be here for Boota. Then we leave, and we should be back by two weeks' time, give or take."

He nodded. "So who else will be coming with us?"

I drew in a sharp breath, knowing what he meant. "No one can come, can they?" We were going to Maledicta Terra, one of the most dangerous of lands on the planet. I wanted Gustav to come, but I knew that if something were to happen to him, I would never forgive myself for it.

He shook his head. "No one but us can go."

I turned to face him, catching his pale magenta eyes. They used to be full of light, but now they were just eerie. "We will in two days then."

Just then, someone came crashing through the library doors, sending us jumping into fighting stance. I relaxed immediately when I saw it was Aleks. "Jesus, Aleks, would it kill you to knock? And why aren't you with Boota?"

He had a bewildered expression, and his voice came out unusually high. "We have a problem. Someone came for a visit."

"Who?" both Siddiqis and I asked at the same time.

"You should come and see for yourselves." He turned away and went running through the library doors, his footsteps echoing through the hallway.

I looked at Siddiqis, and we both started running after Aleks. In less than ten seconds, we caught up to him as he ran into the castle's foyer.

I grabbed Aleks's arm and pulled him to face me. "What's going on?"

His voice came out uneven. "See for yourself." He gestured with his free hand to the meeting hall.

I peered at him for a second, and then I walked toward the meeting hall doors and threw them open.

I felt as if a cold winter breeze had hit my very core, freezing me in place. "Aries?"

Aries smiled from his seat at the table. "Kyra!"

"Wh-what are you doing back so early?" I stuttered.

He got up and walked over, giving me a confused face. "I told you I'd be back in a week, remember?"

Everyone in the room looked at me from behind Aries's back, wide-eyed, and I mentally smacked myself. I had been unconscious for five days. Crap. "Oh, um, I forgot," I blurted out. My voice cracked; that never happened before.

Aries looked around at everyone and then behind my shoulder. "Aleks, what's wrong?"

I peered over my shoulder to Aleks then darted my eyes from him to Siddiqis, who was hiding from Aries's view, away from the doorway. Aleks understood. "Nothing. Really, we just lost track of time–"

"Aleks, tell me the truth."

"The truth?" he squeaked, and I knew why Aries was asking Aleks; he couldn't lie at all. While everyone had a poker face on, Aleks looked nervous and was fidgeting.

I piped in. "Aries, really, there's nothing–"

"I'm asking Aleks," he interrupted with a tone that made me shut up. He narrowed his eyes at Aleks, and everyone stared at Aleks with a stare that said "Don't screw up." "Aleks, the truth. Now."

Aleks looked ready to faint, and I was pretty sure he was about to.

"It's okay. I got this," sighed Siddiqis, his eyes on Aleks. He emerged in front of the doorway, walking past Aleks, who was wide-eyed, and stood next to me, staring at Aries. "Hello, Aries." He waited cautiously, examining Aries's every movement.

Aries stood still for a moment. Then as if time had fast-forward, he was across the foyer, with his hands around Siddiqis's neck.

I was suddenly thrown into the wall next to Siddiqis, the connection at work. I gasped at the sudden pain, taken by surprise.

Gustav yelled. "No! Father, stop! You're–"

But it was too late. I was being choked through the connection, and blue spots appeared before my vision. The lack of oxygen in my head made me dizzy, and I fought for air, fighting the invisible force.

Aries, seeing what was happening to me, suddenly let go of Siddiqis's neck, stumbling backward and looking at the two of us with a startled expression.

Siddiqis and I fell to our knees beside each other, letting out a coughing fit. He caught his breath first, and he turned to me, one hand on my back, another gripping my arm to keep me steady as I kept coughing. Finally, I stopped and just stayed there to get my heart beating back to normal. When I was all right, I started to stand, and so did Siddiqis, who still held my arm and back.

We got to our feet and looked at Aries, who was shocked and horrified. Everyone stood in the foyer, staring at me with concern. I cleared my throat. "I'm good. Don't worry." I looked over at Siddiqis, who was staring at Aries with a deadly look.

Aries finally found his voice and spoke slowly but with intense frustration. "Someone better tell me what's going on right now."

Everyone exchanged glances nervously, and I stared at Siddiqis, just in case he was planning on doing something stupid.

Finally, Darq spoke in an almost humorous voice. "The baby's born."

Aries whipped around to face Darq, confused. "What?"

"The baby, Boota's and mine. He's been delivered. Just a while ago. We named him Mason." Darq looked unsure whether he should smile or whether it was a bad time to have brought up the matter.

Aries's mouth dropped open, but he quickly recovered and turned his head to look at me. "We'll talk about this later."

I nodded silently, still shaken by what had just occurred.

Suddenly, there was the whooshing of air, and Aries was suddenly running up the stairs two steps at a time. Everyone except for Aleks, Siddiqis, and I went after him, probably to explain the situation for me after he saw Mason.

Aleks walked over to me and sighed. "I choked."

My mouth set itself automatically into a tight straight line. "Yeah. I know." I slowly pulled away from Siddiqis, and he made no move to stop me.

Aleks then looked at Siddiqis with an uneven expression. "Look, I'm sorry I choked. Maybe if I told him–"

"Save your breath," Siddiqis interrupted with a sigh. "We both know that either way, he would have attempted to kill me. I was just getting irritated by watching you stutter."

Aleks crossed his arms over his chest defensively. "Can't you just stop with the 'I don't give a crap' attitude?"

I groaned, massaging my temples. "Okay, let's not do this right now, guys. I need some air." I walked to the front doors, pulling them open and letting them close behind me.

I took a deep breath in and exhaled, enjoying the refreshing cool air. Despite it being April, the weather was still quite frosty, though the flowers were in full bloom. Everything was calm and soothing–perfect even.

Then the perfectness shattered as I shouted out at the sharp pain in my head. This migraine was getting worse. I felt dizziness set in, and I blinked a few times to get my vision straight. I decided to go to the castle infirmary to check what was wrong with me and to possibly get some aspirin.

I opened the front doors again and saw the two boys were nowhere in sight. I made my way through the castle to the infirmary and closed the door behind me.

Urani Lander stood by a table, folding the freshly cleaned white sheets. When she looked up and saw it was me, she curtsied. "Hello, Your Highness. How may I help you?"

She had a nasal tone, though was pretty and delicate as a flower. Her hair was in her famous fishtail braid, which she wore daily, and she had soft round brown eyes. Her skin wasn't tanned or pale. Her mouth was always in a polite smile.

I returned her smile. "I would like you to check me for any illnesses. I'm afraid I've been having a massive headache, as well as dizziness."

She smiled. "Of course, Your Highness. Please take a seat and lie back." She motioned at a table where a cloth was spread out on the surface.

I did as I was told and lay on my back slowly.

Urani Lander was a witch as well as the infirmary's head nurse. She placed her hands on my temples and instructed me to close my eyes. When I closed them, I heard her breathing deeply and felt the throbbing pain soon diminish.

I sighed with my eyes closed, happy. "It's gone. Thank you—"

Urani gasped, and I felt her hand pull away from my temples as if I had shocked her. My eyes flew open, and I sat up, peering at her with slight concern. "What's wrong?"

She stared at me, stunned. "Your Highness, I had a vision when I placed my hands on your head."

"What did you see?" I asked slowly.

She didn't look horrified or happy; she just stood there, rigid and shocked. "You're pregnant."

# CHAPTER 16

## Issues

THOSE TWO WORDS were enough to leave me stunned. I sucked in a tight breath and slowly exhaled, trying to grasp my head around this situation.

I thought back to those days and months before Siddiqis had come back, and then it struck me: I missed my period. It came back in shards of memories: that night Gustav and I made love near the end of March. I missed my period, which was supposed to come early April. The vomiting, the dizziness—it all made sense now. Those were all signs of early pregnancy.

Now, a few minutes later, I looked over from my place on the table to the positive pregnancy test, gripping the edge. "I'm an idiot."

Urani sighed. "Your Highness, it's all right to be pregnant. You're going to be a mother—"

"But you don't understand, Urani. I must go away in two days' time."

Her eyes went wide. "Oh no, Your Highness. You can become ill, and you're going to be weak since now you're eating for two."

Eating for two, I repeated in my head. I was already shaking my head. "I must go. I'll be careful, but I'll need you to do me two favours."

She looked ready to argue but reluctantly nodded. "Anything."

"First off, you must promise me that you will not speak a word to anyone about this. I cannot alarm anyone. We're already in panic. Second of all, I need you to tell me what to do before I leave so I'm prepared for what will happen. God knows how long I'll be away."

She bit her bottom lip. "Does that include not telling the rest of the royal family, Your Highness?"

"Yes. I'm afraid it'll be too much for them to bear. Will you do me those two favours?"

She was hesitant but reluctantly agreed. "But you must be very careful, Your Highness. You carry another life in you, and I have a feeling the child will be extraordinary."

"Don't worry. I'll be okay." I got up to leave and decided I had enough of the day. "I think I'll go to my room and rest until tomorrow morning."

"If you would like, I can send some servants up to serve you breakfast and your meals in bed."

"No, that's all right, Urani. I must keep attending the meals with the others so they don't get suspicious."

"All right . . . but may I tell you something?"

"Of course."

"Well, I have the gift of knowing early on if an unborn child is male or female." She smiled. "It's a girl."

I looked down at my stomach. Of course I hadn't gotten a huge baby bump yet, but I was able to make out the quiet beating of an infant's heart. A girl, I thought, smiling. She'd probably be a fighter like her mother.

I looked back up to Urani's smile. "Thank you."

She blushed. "No problem, Your Highness."

"Please, call me Kyra."

She went even redder.

I left the infirmary and decided it was time to call it a day. With everything that was going on, my head wouldn't stop spinning, and I feared that if I didn't sleep, I would faint and might hurt the baby.

I made my way to Gustav and my room, closing the door behind me. I turned and shrieked.

Aleks stood a few feet away from me. "Sorry, Kyra. I didn't mean to startle you."

I breathed in and out deeply, a hand over my heart as I tried to calm my racing heart. "It's all right. I've just been a little jumpy lately," I lied.

He nodded. "Um, I wanted to talk to you about something."

"Sure." I gestured to the couches in the sitting room. We sat side by side. "What's up?"

He bit his bottom lip. "Well, you see, um, in the past few days, I've been noticing something strange about you."

"Um, okay?"

"And I think that you might be pregnant."

My mouth dropped open. "What?"

"It's just, I heard you vomited this morning, and you've seemed to be really weak, and Siddiqis told me your powers are weakening, and that's usually a sign of pregnancy for hybrids." He looked down. "And I've heard another heartbeat besides yours. Like, a super quiet one but a strong beat."

Crap, I thought. So much for not telling anyone. I sighed. "Aleks, you can't tell anyone."

He jumped to his feet, suddenly. "Wait. You really are pregnant!" he nearly yelled.

"Shhh. Keep it down. Only you, a nurse, and I know about this."

He gawked. "Kyra, you're pregnant, for God's sake!"

"Yeah, I know!"

"For how long did you know?"

"I just found out a few minutes ago, Aleks."

"Oh my god, you're pregnant!" This time he said it with awe and excitement.

I smiled softly. "Yeah, I am. It's a girl, apparently."

"That's wonderful–"

"And I'm leaving this Friday."

A silence passed, and Aleks went rigid. Then he slackened and fell back into the couch. He spoke slowly. "Where?"

I looked down at my hands in my lap. "Maledicta Terra."

He gawked at me. "You can't be serious."

"I am. It's apparent that the only way to break this bond is to find the mysterious Prophecy Sisters, and this book that Siddiqis found about how the prophecies are created said that they can be summoned in the Cursed Caves, which is in–"

"Maledicta Terra." He ended my sentence with a groan.

"Yeah," I sighed.

"What did Gustav say about this?"

"Nothing, because he doesn't know about the trip or about her." I rubbed my belly absently to soothe the baby within me.

Aleks leaned back and swiped a hand through his hair, a habit from long ago. "Oh god, Gustav will freak out. So will the others. Am I the only one who knows?"

"I told you before, you, Urani Lander, the nurse who told me about the pregnancy, and I."

He groaned again. "Kyra, you need to tell Gustav."

I also leaned back, trying to push the rising headache out of my pile of issues. "If I do tell him now, he won't let me go to Maledicta Terra."

"What makes you think I'll let you go there?" he muttered, loud enough for me to hear.

I raised an eyebrow. "Aleks, let's be clear about one thing. We both know that the only way you're going to stop me from going is by hurting me to the point I can't move, and we both also know that you won't do a thing to harm a pregnant woman, nonetheless your friend and her to-be-born child."

He slowly looked over at me, his face unreadable. "Rumblen, don't go there with me."

Oh boy. He only used my middle name when we fought. "Aleks, there's nothing you can do, all right? I'm linked to Siddiqis. That means if he dies, I die. That would mean the child I carry also dies. This is the only shot. And even if you tried, you won't be able to stop me."

He jumped to his feet and loomed over me, his hands now braced on either side of my head, gripping the couch's frame behind me. His face was expressionless. "Kyra, you're right that won't hurt you or the baby, but I swear to God, if the only way to keep you from going is to restrain you, I will do so, because I will not let you hurt this child and yourself." His eyes flashed with something that looked like calm rage. "I'm not the shy, awkward guy I once was. I've gotten stronger, and because you are pregnant, you are getting weaker. Don't test me."

I was stunned. "Aleks Silvermoon, you did not just say you will restrain me."

He tilted his head slightly. "I just did, Kyra Rumblen Deatheye."

We glared each other down for a full minute until the bedroom door openned and Gustav's voice boomed through the room. "Kyra?"

Aleks made distance between us, and I got to my feet. "In here, Gustav," I called to him.

Aleks leaned beside me to whisper in my ear, "We will talk about this later." Then he glided past Gustav, out the door, leaving the air filled with static.

Well, that escalated quickly, I thought.

Gustav gave me a questioning look. "What was that about?" He jabbed a thumb toward where Aleks had stormed off.

I waved my hand. "Nah, it's all right. We just had a small argument."

"About what?"

"Um, I'll tell you later. But there's something I need to tell you now."

"Okay."

I walked toward him and then took both his hands in mine. They were made to fight with a sword, but I still admired them.

"Gustav, Siddiqis and I found a way to break the bond." I took in a sharp breath. "We need to go to Maledicta Terra."

His eyes went wide with stun. "No."

"Yeah." I explained what we had learned and left out the part of my pregnancy.

"I'm going with you."

"No, Gustav. I need to do this alone with Siddiqis."

"Kyra, you do realize that you're saying you want to go on a two-week trip with the guy that killed you once and still wants you dead, right?" His eyes searched mine for an explanation.

"I know, Gustav, and I don't like it either. But the Prophecy Sisters strike down any person who tries summoning them except hybrids."

He looked down at our linked hand and sighed. "There's no way at all beside this?"

I shook my head. "There's no other way."

He looked up at me and nodded. "Fine. I feel like an idiot agreeing with this, but if this is the only way you and the freak will be separated, then I guess you will have to go." He then embraced me into a tight hug and whispered in my ear. "Please be careful."

I hugged him back. "I will," I whispered back, pushing back tears that threatened to appear.

We broke our embrace, gave each other a peck on the lips, and then headed to bed. I changed out of my outfit into a baggy shirt and shorts then climbed into bed.

As I lay there beside Gustav, hearing his rhythmic breathing against my neck, my back to his chest, I wondered what was I going to do. A girl, I numbly thought. I had to break the bond, not just for myself, but for my daughter as well.

*****

I awoke the next morning to the banging at the door of the bedroom. I heard Gustav wake up as well, and he jumped out of bed to answer the door.

As I sat up, I raised a hand to my eyes, squinting at the morning light. When my eyes adjusted, I saw it was Aries. Oh boy, I thought as Gustav back up while Aries walked into the room, closing the door behind him.

Aries had a white T-shirt on with black track pants. Images suddenly flashed in my mind: Aries in a suit and tie every day. It was weird that he was wearing such mundane clothing. "What's wrong, Aries?"

He looked at Gustav. "Give me a moment with Kyra please."

Gustav gave me a questioning look as well as a "good luck" look we shared whenever Aries wanted to talk to one of us alone. He walked out of the bedroom, his footsteps echoing in the scarce hallway, and Aries closed the door.

"What did I do?" I asked.

He turned around, and his eyes dropped to my stomach and then to my eyes. "You tell me."

I stood rigid. "How did you know?"

"Aleks. He told me last night before bed and said that only you, a nurse, him, and I know." His black onyx eyes stared me down. "I didn't hear Gustav's name in that list of people."

"Aries–"

"And then he told me you were planning on leaving to go to Maledicta Terra with Siddiqis." He was now fuming.

Oh lord. "Aries, you don't understand. I either go or stay stuck with Siddiqis."

"Kyra, have you ever wondered what will happen if you died?"

"Yes, I have, but right now, I'm mainly focused on getting this over with so I can be a mother in peace."

"If you don't make it out, you will already be dead along with my to-be-granddaughter!" His voice was slowly rising to a shout.

"And if I don't do this, then the next time I get hurt, I'll lose the child!" I yelled back.

He stood silent and then spoke quietly. "I shouldn't upset you." He looked back down at my stomach. "The child shouldn't get upset."

I also looked down at the small baby bump that had just developed overnight. "Aries, can you get me Urani Lander?"

"Why–"

"Aries, please just get her. And don't tell the others. I'll tell them after the trip."

His face fell, but nodded. "Fine. I'll get her, and you can go. But if you don't come back, I don't know what we will all do without you." He gave me a brief peck on the cheek. "We already lost you once, Kyra." He whispered in my ear, "We won't lose you again." Then, just like that, he left the room, leaving me with the sound of a child's heartbeat.

# CHAPTER 17

## Visitors

"YOU WILL DEFINITELY need lots of food. Maybe you should start using blood bags, since the child will also be part vampire, and blood will give you more strength."

I gawked at Urani. "I haven't had blood for a year now."

"Well, now is the time to get the habit back. Don't drink blood straight from the vein though. It'll make you throw up. Better to bring lots and lots of blood bags."

I sighed but wrote "Blood bags" on the list of things to bring. Right after Aries had left, I started vomiting yet again, and Urani arrived just in time with medicine to stop the vomiting. Tomorrow, I would be leaving, and I wanted to make sure I had everything I needed to keep the child healthy. "What else?"

She pursed her lips together. "That's everything. What did you write down?"

I looked down at the list and recited the list to her aloud. "Pair of baggy clothes with war gear, toothbrush and toothpaste, inflatable pillow, medicine to stop vomiting that I should take before bed and in the morning, special ointment for headaches, and blood bags." I looked back up to her. "Did I miss anything?"

"No. Now you're ready. Just be careful, try not to get hurt, and the blood bags will help with your powers, since they are fading because of the pregnancy."

"Also, Urani, because of my hybrid status, is there a possibility the baby may come earlier than planned?"

She blinked, considering what I said, and chose her words carefully. "It's very unlikely. Yes, you will get a small baby bump, but no, the baby shouldn't be coming anytime soon."

I exhaled in slight relief. "Well, at least I won't be in labor when I'm away."

She nodded, but a weighing feeling came off her.

"What's wrong?"

"It's just, if you don't return, what will we do?" Her eyes were pinched with tears.

I got up and hugged her. "I will. Don't worry," I assured her. Then I released her from the embrace. "I need you to help the others as well while I'm gone."

She nodded vigorously. "Of course, anything."

I thanked her, and as she closed the door behind her, I stood facing the window, watching the town from a distance come alive. It was almost 1:00 p.m., and I had eaten the waffles Urani had brought up earlier, and the medicines I took had worked.

I let out a sigh. Being pregnant was harder than I had expected.

A knock came from the door. Without turning, I called, "Come in!"

I heard the door open and close as he walked in. "You ready for tomorrow?"

I turned my head to the sound of Siddiqis's voice. "Yeah." I turned fully around and wasn't fazed by the sight of him shirtless and his snug denim jeans. He had taken a shower; drops of water dripped from his hair. I frowned. "You're dripping on the carpet."

"Oh. My bad." Without asking, he went into Gustav's and my bathroom and grabbed a towel to dry his hair.

He looks so young, I realized, and then my eyes dropped to the scar right where his heart was.

He caught me staring and winced as if I had slapped him. "Thinking of the old times, are we?"

The memory was still vivid in my head: the last kiss I gave him and the moment I stabbed right through his heart. "Yeah, I guess you can say that."

He bit his lip. "Do you still have your scar?"

I was hesitant but then pulled down the neck of my shirt, exposing the scar that I had tried so hard to rid myself of but wouldn't leave. "Still got it."

He came close enough for me to smell the lemony scent of his body soap and slowly felt the scar. At first, I was going to flinch but decided otherwise. There was no reason for me to be afraid of him; I could still take him, pregnant or not. I stood still while he inspected the scar that he had made a year ago.

Then I gave into my urge and felt his scar. He didn't flinch either, and both of us stood closer than before, eyeing the wounds we had inflicted to each other. By the looks of his scar, which looked identical to my own, it wasn't going to fade away.

I cleared my throat and stepped away from him. He also took a step back, and we exchanged silence.

Then his eyebrows furrowed together, and he looked down at me with a questioning gleam in his magenta eyes. "Do you hear that?"

"Hear what?"

"It sounds like…" He paused. "It sounds like a child's heartbeat."

Crap. "What?" Crap. "Your hearing is probably off again, or maybe you're overhearing Laylita's kid."

"No, I heard a child's heartbeat in this room." He closed his eyes and focused on the sound, and if I didn't act now, he would've found out about my pregnancy.

So I punched him. The impact made a horrible smack, and I felt Siddiqis's nose break with a sickening crack.

"Aggghhhhhhhhhh!" he yelled out, as well as a very unintelligible stream of words, while his hand flew up to his face to hold his poor broken nose. "What the–"

Suddenly, I felt a massive invisible impact in my nose as it broke. "Aghhhhhhhhh!" I mentally kicked myself; I had forgotten about the bond. Idiot. "I didn't mean to hit you that hard!"

"What was that for!"

"I saw a mosquito on your nose and panicked," I lied and silently cursed myself for coming up with a lame excuse like that. I held a hand up to my nose and winced in pain as I attempted to push it back in place so it could heal.

He was trying to keep calm; he spoke slowly. "You punched me in the face ... because you saw a freaking mosquito?" His voice rose into a shout, and I stood cautiously away from him.

"I'm sorry, okay!" I shouted back.

"I didn't even hear a mosquito!"

"Well, I saw it, and you were kind of occupied, so at least I saved you a mosquito bite!"

"You broke my nose!" If he were a cartoon character, he would've had steam coming out of his ears.

Oh lord. "I said I was sorry!"

"Kyra, why–"

The bedroom door banged open, and Aleks came running in. "What the heck is going on?" He looked at me but quickly averted his gaze to Siddiqis, who was now struggling to keep his cool. "What happened?"

Siddiqis, with one hand over his nose, gestured with his other hand toward me. "Ask her!" He walked over to the bathroom door and slammed it shut, still grumbling obscenities.

Aleks turned his gaze then to me, with one eyebrow raised. "What did you do?"

I glanced down to the floor. "He heard the baby's heartbeat, and before he could hear it was from me, I punched him. I didn't mean to go that hard on him."

Aleks sighed. "Why don't you tell him?"

"Oh yeah, sure. I should totally tell the guy who wants to kill me that I'm pregnant right before we go on a trip alone where he can murder me. Nice plan, Aleks," I said sarcastically.

He held up his hands. "Hey, I heard people screaming, and so I came. I'll be going now." He began to walk to the door.

"Wait! Aleks!" I called.

He stopped and turned to face me, an impatient look on his face.

"Um, I can't push my nose back into its place, and if I don't get it in place, it won't heal. So can you, um . . ." With my spare hand, I motioned to my nose.

"Oh. Um, sure." He came back to me and took in a sharp breath as he pulled my hand away from my nose. "Wow, you punched him hard."

"Yeah, I kind of know that now."

"Okay, um, this is going to hurt." He took deep breaths and held my nose with one hand, making me wince in pain, and supported the back of my head with the other hand.

His eyes were wide. "Ready?"

"Just do what you got to do." I groaned, clenching and unclenching my fist.

He nodded. "Okay, on three." He took in a deep breath. "One, two–"

"What's going on?" Gustav had walked through the door right when Aleks abruptly pushed my nose back into place.

I shrieked with pain.

Aleks let me go, and I went to hold my nose, this time in more pain. "I told you it would hurt!"

I waved my spare hand. "Yeah, I just didn't think it would hurt like that."

Gustav rushed over to me. "What the–"

"Kyra, I need you to put my nose back in place," said Siddiqis as he walked out of the bathroom and then saw Gustav and Aleks. "Or, you know, one of you can help me undo what she did."

Gustav looked around and shouted. "Can someone tell me what's going on!"

Aleks started backing up. "I was just leaving." He shot me a look that said "Good luck," and then he was gone out the door.

Gustav turned to face me, and I sighed. "I saw a mosquito on Siddiqis's nose and hit it but accidentally broke both of our noses, but Aleks pushed mine back into place." I gestured at my now healed yet sore nose. "See? Good as new."

Siddiqis grunted. "Um, a little help please?" he said in a nasal-like voice.

I walked over to him and placed one hand on his nose and the other at the back of his head. "Ready?"

"Yeah. Just try to be–"

I pushed his nose back in place before he could finish his sentence.

He pulled away from me, shouting a colourful swarm of obscenities.

Gustav sighed. "Kyra, you up for training?"

I was about to respond yes until I remembered: it's not good to fight while being pregnant. "Rain check? I have to pack up for the trip."

He tried to hide his disappointment, but I caught a glance of it. "Okay. I'll be training alone, I guess." And with that, he was gone, leaving Siddiqis and me alone.

Siddiqis recovered and gave me a look. "Since when have you ever rejected training?"

I sighed. "Since I realized I need to pack for the big trip. We are going to be away for a long time." I ushered him out the door. "You should get packing." I explained quickly, pushing him out the door.

I tried closing the door, but he caught it and held it open. "Are you all right? You've been acting weird lately." He narrowed his magenta eyes at me with suspicion.

"Yeah, I'm okay. Just a little nervous about the trip, that's all." It was, in fact, part of the truth.

He looked down and then at me. "To be honest, I am too." With that, he let go of the door and walked away.

I closed the door and sagged against it. Tomorrow I would be gone. The day after that, I could end up dead. *Just pack your things, Kyra*, I thought to myself and walked to my closet with the list of things I needed, slightly trembling in my hands.

*****

A knock from the door made me lose count of the blood bags I had packed. "Come in!" I called from my place next to my bed where I was filling my duffel bag with the things I needed.

I heard the door open and close, and I looked up just in time to see Boota come in, carrying Mason in a blue blanket.

I smiled. "Hey. How's our little Deatheye doing?"

She returned the smile. "He's been quiet and hasn't been a handful at all." She nodded at the bed. "Packing for the trip?"

"Yeah. I was going to tell you about the trip later today."

"Aries has already told everyone in the castle that you are leaving with Siddiqis for a trip to Maledicta Terra." Her eyes showed her worry. "Are you sure you should be going?"

I nodded and kept my mouth in a straight line. "I have to go. If it's the only way to break this bond, then I have to, Boota."

She nodded, and I then realized how thick the air around us became. I walked over to her and placed a hand on her shoulder. "Boota, are you all right?"

"Not really, Kyra. It's just, what if when Mason grows older and he turns out to be rogue and doesn't care about anything?" she admitted, eyes full of thoughts.

I sighed. "Boota, he is a dark angel. He won't have many feelings, yes. But we can help him and make sure he doesn't act without reason. Everything will be fine." I smiled to reassure her.

She nodded. "I just don't want him going down the wrong path." She stared down at the child in her arms, who was asleep.

I also examined Mason. He was strikingly beautiful, and he looked less maleficent when asleep. He was going to be the brightest star in Darq's and Boota's night; that was for sure.

I looked back up at Boota. "I should keep packing. And you need to go get some sleep."

She smiled, nodding. "Yeah. Just don't leave before saying good-bye." She then left the room, and I went back to packing the blood bags, trying to fantasize what might happen on the trip I was going to endure tomorrow.

## CHAPTER 18

### Farewells

THURSDAY WENT BY in a blur, and Friday was already upon us. I had my duffel bag packed up with blood bags, clothing and war gear, water bottles, medication, painkillers, and everything I needed, including weapons and an updated map that weren't originally on the list but I had decided to be safe than sorry. I wore my extra pair of war gear: black tights, black tank tops with a black leather vest with multiple zippers, and black boots. I was able to move freely in them and they weren't uncomfortable at all.

It was Friday morning when Siddiqis met up with me in the castle's foyer, and we exchanged nods. I cleared my throat. "Do you have everything?"

"Yep." He gestured to his own backpack. "I pretty much packed water and first-aid things, as well as clothing, a map, and weapons. Oh, and I'm bringing along that history book on the Prophecy

Sisters to help us just in case." He too was wearing traditional war gear: black pants, black shirt, and black boots as well.

"Good."

We exchanged an awkward silence, both looking down at our feet.

"You guys ready?" said Angela, who made her way toward us down the stairs, wearing a high-low skirt and a short-sleeved white shirt.

I looked up at her and forced an even smile. "Yeah, we are."

She came toward me and embraced me tightly, and I hugged her back as well. "You better come back, girl," she mumbled in my hair.

I nodded. "I will," I mumbled back and then let her go, holding her at arm's distance. "I'll be back. I promise."

Her eyes gleamed but with sadness. "You always keep your promises." She quickly swept a hand over her eyes to stop incoming tears from falling. "Make sure you don't break this one."

My throat went dry at this, so I nodded numbly.

Then Aleks, Laylita, Gustav, Stefan, Boota carrying Mason, Darq, Aries, and Urani came down the stairs toward us.

Stefan muttered "Good luck" to both Siddiqis and me and waited by the stairs.

Darq, in a flannel shirt and jeans, and Laylita, in a flowing blue dress, embraced me and wished me good luck, while shaking hands with Siddiqis as they wished him good luck as well.

Aleks, wearing dress pants and a shirt, pulled me into a long embrace. "Be careful, Kyra," he said, tears pinching his eyes and his voice cracking.

I sniffled, pushing tears of my own back. "I will."

Then Boota, looking petite in a cardigan and jeans, handed Mason to Aries and embraced me tightly. "What are we going to do without you?" she asked in a shaky voice as she pulled away, tears slipping down her cheeks.

I couldn't help it; a tear slipped down my own cheek. "I'll be back as soon as the bond is broken. I swear I'll be back."

She nodded and then took Mason back from Aries and held him out to me.

I took the infant in my arm and peered down in his sharp eyes. "Don't do anything too amazing without me here please." I chuckled a little when he giggled at that and grabbed for my platinum lock of hair. "Not that hard and emotionless, are you now?" I kissed his forehead and handed him back to his mother.

As Boota went to Darq, Aries, in a suit as usual, stepped forward and hugged me lightly. "Do you have everything you need?" he whispered so only I could hear.

"Yeah."

"Just promise me that you will take care of yourself and my to-be-born hybrid grandchild. If you do just that, I'll promise you that I won't worry as much as I know I will." His black eyes were struggling to look serious in the saddening moment we were in.

I vaguely remember the last time they were filled with tears: the day Siddiqis killed me and brought back my body to the castle and how Aries had cried his heart out.

I smiled sadly. "I promise, Aries. I promise."

He exhaled, and with a nod, he stepped away, and as soon as he did so, Gustav swept me off my feet and clutched me closely to his body, his arms around my waist, his breath ragged against the side of my neck.

I wrapped my arms around his neck and let the tears come down silently. We stayed like this for a full minute, taking in each other's feelings and clutching each other as if the other were about to disappear into thin air.

His voice shook, and his words were choked. "Do you not remember what you swore to me? That day on the battlefield when we had won the battle against Siddiqis? Do you remember what you swore to me?"

I nodded, it all coming back to me. "I'd never leave you, never again. But I'll be back, Gustav."

He placed me back to the ground and loosened his grip just to look me in the eyes and held a hand to my wet cheek, his own eyes wet. "I can't lose you again, Rumblen."

I placed my hand over his and weakly smiled. "You won't."

He pulled me into a passionate kiss, both crushing my lips and numbing any fear I felt before. My hands ran through his hair, and his arms wrapped around my waist as we pushed up against each other, and the more we kissed, the more the kisses became less passionate and more frantic, both of us keeping in mind how it might be the last we would share.

It reminded me of the first kiss we shared, where he explained why he was so cold to me before we had even properly met. I fell in love with him all over again and wished the kiss wouldn't have to stop.

But it had to, and so we both pulled away and said our goodbyes to each other, never breaking eye contact until he turned away to take his place beside Aries.

Urani then stepped forward and whispered to me, "I'll take care of Ms. Howls and remember to take the medication."

"I will. Thank you for everything, Urani."

She bit her lip. "Kyra, I wasn't planning on telling you in fear it may affect you or the child, but you should know that when I saw Siddiqis, I had a vision."

I looked around, and everyone seemed busy talking to one another, and Siddiqis was in deep thought. Then I leaned toward Urani. "What did you see, Urani?" I asked quietly.

Her eyes were wide with what I thought looked like fear. "I saw Siddiqis holding a year-old baby boy." She paused. "The child and Siddiqis looked so alike, and I got the feeling that the child was a hybrid as well, but stronger."

My jaw dropped a little. "You think that Siddiqis has—"

"A child that no one knows about? Yes. I think that's exactly the case."

I nodded, letting it sink in. "That explains where he was a year ago before his welcome party here at the castle."

"What should I do with this information?"

I thought for a moment. "Find out where this child is. Don't tell anyone though."

She nodded and wished me farewell.

I turned to the crowd of friends and family that gathered to see me out on the trip Siddiqis and I were about to embark. They were all turned toward us, with tears glistening in their eyes.

I surprised myself by how even my tone actually sounded. "We will be back soon with this bond broken. Please take care of the kingdoms together and don't panic. The kingdoms cannot know of this trip, or else they will be put into lockdown mode." I smiled, tears in my eyes blurring my vision. "Good-bye for now, friends."

They all said good-bye, and with that, I looked at Siddiqis, who was staring at me with a look I wasn't able to decipher. "Ready?" I asked.

He nodded. "Ready."

We both grabbed our duffel bags and headed out through the front door, making our way to the Jeep that was waiting in the front for us.

Siddiqis climbed into the driver's seat, and I sat in the front beside him. He turned the engine on, and we were on the road, on our way to our possible freedom or to our possible death.

We drove in silence for a few minutes, and finally, I broke the silence. "So where are we headed right now?" I pulled out a pair of sunglasses and placed them over my eyes, the tinted lenses relieving the glare of the harsh sunlight from my eyes.

Siddiqis had pulled on sunglasses as well, with a toothpick in between his teeth, and I couldn't tell through the tinted lenses whether he was looking at me. "We should hit an inn by sundown at the edge of Servic, or if we're lucky, an inn at the edge of Jesarala."

I nodded. "Let's do this."

We sat in silence for a long time, and then Siddiqis spoke. "Doesn't this remind you of old times?"

I scoffed and turned away from his so he couldn't see my expression. It did remind me of old times—long road trips with Siddiqis, both of us in his car, driving with the radio on full blast, hair whipping in the wind, and sunglasses with minty toothpicks.

That was the life I had before the big battle, a life that seemed a lifetime away even though it was a few years ago. It was a reminder of the wild, rogue, immature teen I had been; I was no longer that naive teenager. I was now a mature wife, queen of two countries, the most powerful hybrid, and a future mother. I was in no need of being reckless, and I had no plans on repeating past mistakes.

I absently put a hand to my stomach, feeling my child's heartbeat strong and steady. The medication Urani had given me made the baby bump go down and helped stopped the morning sickness. I just had to take it in the mornings right when I woke up.

I looked over at Siddiqis. "Do you mind if I sleep for a while?"

He responded without turning his head. "Go ahead."

"Thanks. Wake me up when we get to the inn or if anything happens."

He nodded, and I leaned my shoulder against the Jeep's door and closed my eyes, listening to the sounds of the road, and I eventually faded into the darkness of sleep.

*****

I woke up the next day, yawning as I sat up in a bed. Wait, a bed? I wondered, and I looked around quickly at the room I was in. The last thing I had remembered was being in the Jeep.

I was in a cozy big room with a fireplace burning and a living room area. From where I was, I saw a small area that looked like a kitchen, and I was sitting in a queen-sized bed.

I was about to get up until I heard the front door open and close, and then Siddiqis emerged from around the corner with a bag of groceries. He was wearing denim jeans today with the same black shirt and boots he wore yesterday.

When he saw that I was awake, he grinned. "Good morning, Sleeping Beauty. How'd you sleep?" He walked over to the curtains and drew them back abruptly, letting in the blinding morning light.

I raised a hand to my eyes, squinting at the bright light, and my fangs peeked out. "Where are we?" I asked around the fangs.

"In an inn at the edge of Jesarala. We spent a lot of time on the road, and you slept through the whole day." He came over to me and sat next to me at the edge of the bed. "You looked so peaceful, and we got here at midnight, so I decided to heroically carry you to the room, and here we are."

I rolled my eyes and retracted my fangs. "On no level are you heroic, Starburn."

He smirked. "Oh, really? What about that time I saved you from the Servic Wolf Clan?"

"They were going to send me back to the castle, but then you came and knocked down their door." I raised an eyebrow.

"Actually, it was your husband who knocked the door down," he corrected.

I waved off the memory. "Let's just get back on the road."

I started to get up, but he pushed me down. "Nope, I am making us breakfast, and then we will go."

I raised an eyebrow. "Why would I eat anything you make?"

"Because unless you want to starve to death, you're going to have to eat what I make." He stood up and went to the kitchen, whistling a tune.

I started to rise up and felt a sharp pain in my stomach, and I instantly looked around frantically for my duffel bag, which rested on a chair not far from the bed. I jumped out, ignoring the pain, and rushed over to the bag, going through it, and finally pulled out the pills Urani had given me. I quickly took one with a glass of water I had by my bedside. It went down smoothly, and just like that, the pain stopped. I heard footsteps headed my way and quickly hid the pills back in my bag.

Siddiqis came back to the bedroom, a cookbook in his hands, staring down at it in deep concentration. "Hey, which do you prefer, omelets with toast or bacon-covered sausages?" He looked up briefly and then looked back up at my position on the ground.

"Um, bacon-covered sausages please."

He continued to stare. "Mind explaining what you are doing on the floor, Sleeping Beauty?"

I ignored what he had called me. "I just thought that I had forgotten something and decided to go through my bag."

"Huh, all right." He gave me a questioning look and then went back to the kitchen.

I exhaled and quickly pulled myself together and then went to the bathroom. I shut the door behind me and examined my reflection.

I looked the same, if not a little more vibrant, and the pills had done better than I had thought; there was no sign of my baby bump, and I wasn't vomiting.

I took a quick cold shower to wake myself up, and then after brushing my teeth and sliding my hair into a ponytail, I emerged out of the bathroom. I heard Siddiqis singing along to a song on the radio, "Any Other Way," the song we used to listen to when we were dating. I cringed at the memory and waltzed into the kitchen. I was stopped dead in my tracks by what I saw.

Siddiqis stood behind the marble island, his back turned away from me while cooking the bacon and sausages. "Baby, when I see you, it's the feel that rises in me. Even when you're gone, the feelings still stay. I know that you won't ever let me, from this love, ever be free. But I wouldn't have it any other way," he sang on pitch, his voice low and seductive in a way, as he did a funny little dance.

I tiptoed closer and leaned my forearms against the island, grinning as I tried not to laugh. He didn't notice me for a long time, and I watched as he continued his little dance.

Finally, he turned off the stove and turned around. When he saw me, he swore, jumping back, and his hands flew onto the hot stove. He let out an even greater stream of swears and then jumped away from the stove onto the island.

I laughed at this now. "Are you okay?"

He stared at me, holding his hands in pain. "You scared me half to death!" he nearly shouted.

I raised my hands, still chuckling. "I was simply enjoying the free show."

He looked pissed, but after a few seconds, his expression softened and he smirked. "It's been a long time since I've heard that song." He gestured at the radio.

I quickly changed the subject. "Let's see your hands."

He was about to argue but then thought better and held them out, palms facing up.

They were slowly healing but not as fast as they should've been. They weren't critically burned, but it looked painful, and chances were that they were numb.

I bit my lip. "Wow, you really got burned."

He scoffed. "Yeah, I know. I still feel pain."

I hesitated. "Would you like me to help heal it fast?"

He looked surprised but quickly pulled himself together. "Oh, um, yeah. That would be great, thanks."

"Okay." I motioned for him to sit on the island facing me and then took one of his hands in my own. It felt almost alien-like to hold his hand, but at the same time, I had the sense of déjà vu. The memory came crisp into my head: I was sixteen, and Siddiqis had been fighting with his father, which had led to his father breaking the bones in his hand.

I held his hand and felt tears pinch the corners of my eyes, as I gazed into his eyes. "Does it hurt?"

He smiled weakly. "Not as much when you hold it."

I looked down at his broken hand and smoothed a finger against his palm, restoring the bones back into place.

He sighed in relief. "Every time we touch, it feels like I'm being touched by an angel."

I smiled and leaned close to him, our faces inches apart. "Really? That's an awfully cheesy line, Starburn," I whispered.

He grinned. "Always, but it's not just that. When I see you, it always seems as if you are wearing a halo. Every time I touch your skin," he said as he cupped my cheek with one warm hand, "it's like touching an angel, and likewise when you touch me. When our hands are joined"–he took my hand in his, fitting together perfectly–"they fit like pieces to a puzzle. And when we kiss . . ." He leaned in and kissed my lip with such delicacy, I shivered with delight. "I feel my spirit rise and our souls intertwine with each other. And I know that we are meant to be."

His magenta eyes were lit up, and not a single trace of his snarky self was left, but the raw emotion of love was the only thing radiating off of him.

I blinked a couple of times and realized what I was doing; I had ended up closer to Siddiqis than I had been before and was staring dazedly into his eyes.

For a while, I couldn't breathe; the memory was so fresh in my mind that it felt as if it had just occurred.

Siddiqis also stared down at me, and I knew by the look on his face, he was recalling the same memory as I was. He had the same raw expression in his eyes as he did in the memory.

I cleared my throat and stepped back, still holding his hand. I quickly healed it and then gave his hand back to him.

We exchanged silence, and finally, he broke the silence with a voice that almost seemed to shake. "We should probably take the food to go."

"Yeah, I'm not that hungry anymore," I mumbled, already turning away to go to the bedroom where he wouldn't see my reddened cheeks. I quickly grabbed my duffel bag and headed back into the bathroom, closing the door and locking it behind me.

I set my bag onto the sink counter and pulled out a blood bag. As soon as I saw the red liquid, my fangs popped out, slightly cutting my lower lip. I tore open the opening of the bag and started to drink the contents, tasting the familiar metallic, cherry-flavored liquid that was once in a person.

I emptied the whole bag in a few gulps and was surprised to feel the old urge to drink more. But I relented, remembering how the urges would just get worse if I drank more than one bag a day. As of now, I was good to go the whole day without anything until tomorrow.

I sighed and then carefully wrapped the bag in toilet paper and threw it into the garbage. It was time to get back on the road.

# CHAPTER 19

## Confessions and Memories

AFTER GETTING READY for the road again, we checked out of the inn and headed out, back in the Jeep.

When we got a few miles away from the inn, I asked Siddiqis, "What's the plan for today?"

He had that stupid toothpick back in his mouth and his shades back on. "We're going to go along the edge of Possull, and then we make our way through Maledicta Terra."

"Sounds good."

We rode in silence for a painful moment, and I was quick to break it. "Let's see what's playing on the radio." I turned it on, and on came "Any Other Way."

We both looked at each other, and I quickly punched it off, throwing us back into silence. Good lord, I thought as we rode on, neither of us saying a peep.

Then about halfway down the edge of Possull, the Jeep stopped suddenly, causing us both to shout in surprise. "What the heck?" I said, looking back out the window, seeing if we had hit anyone. No one was there.

Siddiqis groaned. "I'll check it out."

He got out of the Jeep and then swore. "We've got a flat tire!" he called to me.

"Oh great. Do you have a pump?"

"Nope. We are going to have to walk to the nearest city in Possull, and we'll get someone to tow it back to the castle while we rent another one."

I got out and grabbed my duffel bag. "How far away is the city?"

He pulled out a map from his own bag and peered at it, as well as glanced around us. "Well, it looks like we're about an hour away from the nearest city, which will be Tryli." He checked his watch and then looked up at the sky. "It's 6:34 p.m., so we should be there at 7:34 p.m. without delays."

"All right, let's go then." We left the Jeep in the middle of the road and strayed away from it, onto the grass, but still along the roadside.

We started to talk about how the academy hadn't taught us anything we really needed, and then our topic changed to the future. "So what are you going to do once we get this bond detached?" he asked me.

I pondered on that. "I'll go back to the castle and continue with my life. What about you?"

He pressed his lips together. "My first plan was to just kill you right after." He then looked over at me. "But there's been a change to my plan. Instead, I'll go off to explore the world."

I raised my eyebrows. "Really? That doesn't sound like you at all."

He chuckled. "Yes, well, dying has opened my eyes to some things, and so did . . ." he trailed off.

"And so did what?" I asked.

He was hesitant. "I don't know."

I pushed on, however. "What's the big secret?"

"Nothing."

I decided to attack the situation in a different way. "Why don't we make a deal?"

He looked over at me for a split second and then forward again. "I'm listening."

"How about after we break the bond, there will be peace for at least a month or two, and then we settle what was supposed to end last year? I'm willing to keep that deal as long as you answer one question."

He thought for a second of my proposal. "Hmm, seems promising. What's your question?"

"What has made you more good than evil now?"

He looked ready to deny but then sighed and stopped walking. I stopped as well, and he spoke in a low voice. "This information stays between us, understood?"

I nodded, really meaning it.

He took in a deep breath and then spoke slowly and cautiously. "Do you remember the time I first came to the castle for that stupid welcome party?"

I nodded, wanting him to go on.

"Well, before that, I was with someone, a vampire named Kylie Froth." He ran a hand through his hair. "We had sex, and she wasn't on the pill, and so . . . she got pregnant. The child has already been born, and he's turning two years old this year."

I stood rigid and spoke slowly as well. "You're a father." Damn, Urani was right.

He nodded. "Yeah."

We were both silent. Then I broke the silence. "What's his name?"

He smiled. "Denis. Denis Starburn. But of course, because my last name won't do him any good right now, he's Denis Nrubrats."

"Nrubrats?"

"My last name backward."

"Hmm. It sounds like a name for a Nephilim."

He smirked. "That's what I hoped for. So that he can live a normal life."

"You mean a fake one?" I corrected.

He shook his head. "No. A safe one, Kyra." He smiled sadly. "Can you imagine what it would feel like to grow up without a father and yet have his last name that causes fear and anger to tremble through many? I want to be his father, but I can't be because of what I am. His mother will raise him to be good, but no doubt that if he has my last name, his life will go downhill." He caught my stare. "What?"

I shook my head, smiling. "This is the first time in a very long time that I've ever heard you talk like this."

He sighed. "That's what happens when you become a parent, I guess. I just can't stop thinking about him. All you can think about as a parent is about your child."

I averted my eyes down to my stomach; my unborn child's heartbeat raced like my own. "I suppose so," I replied absently.

He didn't seem to notice; he was busy in his train of thought. "I think that if I tried to see him, the neighbours would attempt at killing me or him. Just because of my title, I cannot see my own heir, my own child. Yes, I never meant to be a father in the first place, but now . . . all I can think about and all I dream about at night is the feeling of his little body in my arms and his bright smile that can light a darkened cave . . ."

I stared at Siddiqis with such astonishment that he chuckled. "I know what you're thinking. This obviously isn't the Siddiqis you knew and grown to hate. I must sound like an idiot or a man struck with the disease of love, but I cannot help it, for now I have someone that will love me even though I am who I am."

I didn't have a response for that, so we walked to Tryli in silence.

When we got there, the first thing we did was finding an inn, and in less than five minutes, we had a room ready for us.

As Siddiqis and I walked through the front door, we both stared at the single queen-sized bed in awkward silence.

Siddiqis cleared his throat. "I can sleep on the couch, if you would like?"

"Um, it's all right, I guess. I call the side closest to the wall, however." I didn't want him getting the sense that I was uncomfortable with him in the same bed as me, and it wasn't like we were going to do anything but sleep.

I quickly went into the bathroom and changed into a tank top and sweatpants, and after making sure the medication was doing fine, which it was, I got out and walked right in on Siddiqis taking off his shirt.

I stared at his back with new eyes. Many viewed flawless backs to be attractive, but to me, it was the flaws that stood out. Siddiqis's back contained memories of torture from his evil father, Lucas, who now lived as king of Possull after leaving his place next to his brother in the Demon Realms.

Though he was considered the nicest of the Demon kings, Lucas was still vile and cruel to many and was especially cruel to Siddiqis. He and my mother weren't the best of friends; however, they had mutual respected thoughts toward each other, which was possibly the only reason I survived a dinner with Siddiqis's family. Memories came rushing to the surface of that dinner:

I had knocked on the castle door, smoothing out my dress. Everything had to be perfect when addressing Lucas.

I remember my mother and father arguing the morning before, and thirty minutes later, they both came in with an invitation in my father's hands, trembling slightly, as he passed it to me in silence.

I remember the shock I had felt when I read the message:

"TO MISS COUNT OF THE MORTAL PORTAL, YOU'VE BEEN INVITED TO DINNER TOMORROW. IT'S BY TIME I'VE MET THE GIRL WHO'S THE BURNING STAR OF MY SON'S NIGHT. I LOOK FORWARD TO SEEING YOU SOON.
–KING LUCAS STARBURN OF POSSULL"

My parents told me it was all right if I declined the offer, but I knew better; no one denies a Demon king, even if he resigned his position in the Demon Realms.

I was slightly nervous because there was never an occasion in which Lucas had ever invited anyone to his castle unless it meant they'd never see daylight again.

A hobgoblin opened the door and stared up at me. "What?" he asked rather rudely with a raspy voice.

I took my shades off and revealed my hybrid's mark. "I am Princess Kyra Rumblen Count, daughter of Curtis Count and Lilith Demonheart. I'm here for dinner with the Starburn family." I smiled thinly, trying my best to be polite.

He eyed me and then bowed. "Of course, right this way, Ms. Count."

We walked through the castle, which was much like my own back at the Mortal Portal, and entered a grand dining room.

Sitting across each other at the far ends of the table were Lucas and Zila Starburn, a mighty former Demon king, and his friendly dark angel wife. Siddiqis sat nearest to his mother, farther away from his father, and Siddiqis's younger sister, Razeil, was sitting by his side in between her father and him.

When I went in, they all turned their heads, and when they saw it was me, they all stood, and Siddiqis's eyes raked down my figure and up, as if he were a sponge and was soaking in my every detail. He was wearing suit, just like his father, and looked stunning as usual.

Lucas cleared his throat and smiled, which made me shiver involuntarily. "Hello, Ms. Count."

I took that as an invitation to take my seat across Siddiqis and Razeil. "Thank you again for inviting me over for dinner, Mr. Starburn," I said politely.

He grinned, and then clapping his hands twice, the servants came in with our meals.

After a while of making small chatter, we had all eaten, and then Lucas turned back to me. "Do you know why I wanted you to come here, Kyra?"

Oh boy, he used my first name. "Um, no?" I took a small sip of blood from my cup.

"I invited you because I wanted to show you something." He motioned at Siddiqis. "Stand up, boy," he commanded.

Siddiqis looked baffled. "Pardon?"

Lucas turned to him and smiled vilely. "I said, stand up, boy."

Siddiqis was hesitant but stood up.

"Now take off your shirt."

"But, sir–"

"I said take it off!" Lucas shouted abruptly, causing both Zila and Razeil to flinch, while I tried to keep a poker face as Siddiqis shrugged off his jacket and slipped off his shirt, revealing his abs and tattoo.

Wait, tattoo? I thought, dumbfounded, as I stared at it longer and realized what it was. He had tattooed my full name over his heart. Actually, the tattoo said, "Kyra Rumblen Starburn." He replaced my last name with his.

I looked up for those purple orbs that were his eyes and saw he was looking down at his hands.

Lucas spoke in a humorous tone, but I could still hear the venom behind it. "Why don't you show her what's in your hands, boy? No use in acting like you had nothing planned."

Siddiqis then acted as if he hadn't heard his father and came around the table to me. I stood up and faced him, confused, and he looked down at the object in his hands that he covered from my sight. "Kyra, I meant to show you the tattoo tomorrow, as well as this." He finally held the object up so I could see, and the sight of it made my heart plummet.

It was a small dark-blue velvet box.

Siddiqis then went down on one knee and opened the box, revealing the dark-blue sapphire ring.

I gasped. It couldn't be. He couldn't be . . .

He inhaled and smiled into my eyes. "Kyra Rumblen Count, I knew you since we were children. We've been to hell and back together. I know we are young, but I also know that I will love you forever. Rumblen . . . will you marry me?"

Zila and Razeil gasped and stood, all stunned.

I stood still, stunned. What was I going to do?

Before I could speak, Lucas started to chuckle and soon he dissolved into a maniacal laugh. "Bravo, boy! I'm truly impressed." He stood up. "But you really don't mean to marry her, do you?"

Siddiqis stood up, glaring at his father. "Of course, I meant it. I love–"

Suddenly, Lucas was right behind Siddiqis and shoved him against a wall. "Say it and I'll make you regret it."

I went to grab Lucas off Siddiqis but was then suddenly thrown by an invisible force across the room. I hit the wall hard. All the air in my lungs was forced out, and I went to the ground in pain, clutching my neck.

"Leave her alone!" Siddiqis yelled and then sputtered when Lucas gripped his neck with one hand, and the other hand had fire floating right above his palm.

Lucas grinned. "Take back what you just said then."

I tried getting to my feet, but it was impossible, and I coughed, trying to regain air in my lungs.

Siddiqis wheezed. "Screw you. You always wanted to ruin my life. But you will not ruin this! I love her!"

Lucas was silent as Zila and Razeil pleaded him to stop what he was doing but didn't dare going near him, knowing what would happen if they did.

Then he smirked. "You love her, do you? Well, let me show you how much it hurts to love so young." He flung Siddiqis across the room, and he thudded right next to me, sputtering and coughing.

I reached out to him. "Siddiqis," I croaked.

He reached out for my hand, but Lucas had crossed the room and stomped down on his wrist. There was a sickening crack as he did so. Siddiqis screamed in such pain it shattered my heart, and Lucas, now having a burning metal branding rod in his hand, held Siddiqis again by the neck with the other and pressed the hot end against the tattoo without hesitation.

Siddiqis's screams could've been heard all the way to the Mortal Portal, and I wanted to look away but couldn't, for the sight was so gruesome it trapped my eyes.

"Stop! Please, I beg of you, stop!" I screamed, causing the lights to flicker.

Lucas pulled the poker away from Siddiqis and let go of his neck, causing Siddiqis to drop to the ground in pain.

He stared at me with fascination as I struggled to my feet, and then I glared at him. My tone was venomous that even a cobra would've flinched at the sound of it. "I will leave now, but keep in mind that I am the respected princess of the Mortal Portal. If you did not approve of me for your son, then you should know that I don't give a damn about your blessing."

I looked down at Siddiqis, who cringed at my solemn expression. "Siddiqis, you know that I love you . . . but—"

"Kyra," he interrupted, "it's okay. I understand."

I nodded, both saddened of declining his proposal but also strangely relieved.

I shook my head, the memory breaking, as I looked up to see Siddiqis staring at me with a raw look, the same look he had at the last inn when we both remembered the past.

His voice was unsteady. "Hey."

"Hi," I squeaked. My eyes went back down to his scar over his heart. Though the stab wound was the most visible mark, I was able to see the faint burn mark over the tattoo.

He caught me staring at it and cringed at the memory but said nothing for a minute. When he spoke, his voice was quiet like a whisper. "It wasn't your fault."

I lowered my eyes. "Of course it was. He always wanted to see you weak and vulnerable, and I was your soft spot," I mumbled.

He said nothing to this and instead said he was going to bed, but I had already known that he wasn't going to deny that I was in fact his greatest weakness.

# CHAPTER 20

## Family Problems

I AWOKE THE next morning with one of Siddiqis's arms over me, his other arm under my head and his hard chest against the back of my head. His warmth radiated onto me, yet I was icy cold. I was frozen against him, unsure of what to do.

We had originally slept on the very edge, away from each other, and now we were practically snuggling. I was suddenly aware that my child's heartbeat was hearable, and I slowly lifted up Siddiqis's arm off me, trying not to wake him up.

I felt him stir behind me and then felt him stiffen. It was clear that he was awake. He quickly pulled away from me and jumped off the bed.

I turned over onto my back and slid up into a sitting position, knees into my chest, arms wrapped around them. "Morning."

He was panting as if he were running. "Morning to you too," he replied in a raspy voice. He didn't make eye contact.

I was flustered. "So . . ."

"We never talk of this again. Agreed?"

"Amen," I muttered and then got up to go to the bathroom. I locked the door behind me and leaned my back against it, taking in deep breaths. Control, Kyra, relax, I urged myself, though it wasn't reassuring. Siddiqis was so close to my stomach. What if he had heard the other heartbeat?

I shook my head. No, he couldn't have. He was fast asleep. I took a few deep breaths, and after I was done brushing my teeth, washing my face, and putting on my battle gear again, I emerged from the bathroom.

Siddiqis was already changed and had a map in his hands, sitting at the small table. He was inspecting it with such intensity I was so sure it was going to grow legs and run for the hills. It didn't, but Siddiqis was staring at one place on the map, and when I cleared my throat, he looked up and smirked, showing no sign of the startle that morning. "Hey."

"What did that map ever do to you?" I asked him in a humorous tone.

He shook his head. "Nothing. Why?"

"You looked about ready to strangle the poor thing."

"Very funny."

"No, but really. What were you staring at?" I came from behind him and peered over his shoulder down at the paper.

It was a detailed map of Possull, up to date as well. It was in perfect condition, except that Siddiqis had circled an area. I looked closer and saw that it was the Starburn Castle, home to the horrid Demon king Lucas Starburn.

I started to speak, realizing his plan. "Siddiqis—"

He cut me off. "It's been years since I've seen him. Years, Kyra! He was horrid, and I bet he celebrated my death. I need him to know I'm alive. I need him to know that I'm still up and kicking." He looked over his shoulder at me with fierce determination in his eyes.

I sighed and took a seat across him. "Siddiqis, your father will strike you down the second he senses you."

"I can take him. I know I—"

"Siddiqis, this is your father that we are talking about." I paused to give him a look. "He's stronger than everybody—"

"Except us! You're the Chosen Hybrid, and I'm the Sinner. We are known to be the two most powerful hybrids of the whole world! Kyra, if we tried, we can take him—"

"I'm not going to make a single move against your father. Don't you remember the last time I met with your father?"

"Of course I do!"

"Then you should understand why I'm hesitant on going anywhere near that castle."

Siddiqis opened his mouth, ready to fire his response, but then he stopped and sighed, his expression softening. "I won't pick a fight, I swear. But I just need to see him."

I pursed my lips but reluctantly nodded. "Fine. But the second I think he's going to attack, we run. Remember, you get hurt, I get hurt."

He nodded, smiling genuinely. "Yeah, sure. All right, let's get ready to hit the road. I got us a Jeep waiting in the front."

We packed up everything and got moving right away after returning our room key. We were less than five minutes away from the castle, and as we drove on, we took note of all that was passing us. Possull wasn't a pretty place, though it looked better than how Xercus looked when I had first arrived there. The citizens weren't cheery, and it seemed like each had their own cloud of darkness that followed them everywhere. Their houses were small and made of brick, each surrounded by fences.

"It's changed so much," Siddiqis muttered as we began to go up the hill where the castle was mounted on top.

"So how do we do this?" I asked, realizing we had no plan.

"I actually just planned on walking right in."

"I don't think that's the best idea."

"Well, what did you have in mind?"

"We knock and wait for someone to answer, and then we demand to see the king."

He sighed, trying to look annoyed, but I saw a glimpse of panic. "That's a boring idea, but it'll do."

We finally pulled up to the front, and we both took in a sharp breath. It was still the same; the castle had a Victorian look to it on both the inside and outside, just like the one in the Mortal Portal and Xercus. There was a grand fountain in the front, and Siddiqis missed it by an inch.

I turned and scowled at him. "Let's not break anything here, shall we?"

He smirked but nodded, and we both got out of the Jeep. When we got to the front doors, Siddiqis took in a deep breath and knocked twice. We stood waiting for what seemed to be forever.

Then one of the doors opened, and we looked down at the hobgoblin that opened it. "What do you want," it asked quite harshly.

Siddiqis grinned. "Bathas! C'mon, you couldn't have forgotten me even if you tried."

The hobgoblin, Bathas, looked at Siddiqis and narrowed its eyes. "How are you–"

"Still alive? You can thank that to Mrs. Deatheye." Siddiqis motioned to me.

Bathas gave me a good stare and I then realized that he had been the hobgoblin to open the door when I first came to the castle for the dinner party. "You're married now?" He didn't wait for a response. "Never mind, I don't care. You wish to see the king?"

Siddiqis and I nodded slowly, and Bathas, without saying a word, turned on the ball of his foot–a slimy foot, might I add–and started walking away. We took that as an invitation to go inside, and we followed Bathas to what looked like a meeting room. In the middle were two chairs, and close to the wall were four thrones for the royals.

As we went in, Bathas said, "I'll go tell the king and queen of your arrival."

As he hurried to go, Siddiqis called after him. "Wait, what about my sister? Where's Razeil?"

Bathas paused and looked over his shoulder at us, a solemn look on his face. "She's dead." And then he left, closing the door behind him.

The two of us stood in silence, and then Siddiqis fell into one of the chairs, his hands over his face. He tried not to show it, but I heard his sobs through his hands.

I softened up. "Siddiqis–"

"Did you know?" he asked abruptly, looking up, as tears glistened in his eyes. His cheeks were damp with tears, and I felt my heart melt.

"I honestly had no idea. If I knew, I would've told you." I sat down on the chair beside him. "I'm so sorry."

He shook his head, as if trying to shake out the news he had just heard. "I'm fine. I can grieve later." He swiped at his eyes and cheeks, clearing away the small tears. "Right now, we have the Demon king to confront."

I nodded, and just then, the doors behind us opened. Siddiqis and I turned around and instantly went frozen.

"I didn't believe Bathas until now." Lucas Starburn chuckled and grinned. "Hello, Ms. Count–"

"Mrs. Deatheye," I corrected expressionlessly.

His eyebrows shot up. "You're married?" He then smirked. "To a Deatheye? I heard the rumor of your marriage to the second eldest prince of Xercus but didn't believe it."

"Well, I speak the truth."

"Indeed. You always have," he muttered and walked into the room.

I noticed then that his wife, Zila, was behind him, and when the doors closed behind them, she followed her husband to their places at the line of thrones. She took the second tallest next to Lucas, who took the tallest. Both wore crowns on their heads and had royal clothing on.

After they were seated, Zila cleared her throat, but her voice was quiet. "Hello, Siddiqis. Hello, Kyra."

I decided to curtsy to be polite, considering I was still considered a princess in their land. Siddiqis however stood still, arms crossed over his chest.

"It's been a while, Mother," he said coldly.

"Yes. It has been, son—"

"Do not call that corpse your son, Zila," barked Lucas, causing Zila to look down with a red face. "He is not our son."

Siddiqis stepped forward, but I grabbed his arm. "Siddiqis, remember your promise," I whispered in his ear.

He nodded slowly and walked around the room, away from the rest of us.

I looked at Lucas, who was wearing a calculating expression now. "Siddiqis only wished for you to see that he is alive. We do not come here to start a fight, for we have our own agenda—"

"Does he know?" Lucas interrupted suddenly.

I cocked my head a little to the side, slightly agitated of being interrupted. "Pardon?"

"Does he know of your little secret?" Lucas pronounced every word slowly.

"Um, I don't think I follow with where—"

I was stopped when I saw his eyes darted from my stomach and back up to my eyes. "I think you do."

Oh no, I thought. Of course, he, of all people, would be able to sense my baby. I tried to hide my shock.

It was clear I hadn't covered it well; he grinned. "Aha! I knew it the second you walked in. Oh, how it was so easy to hear and the way you look now. You have a protective edge, one that you didn't have before." Lucas got off his throne and began to circle around me, like a shark circling its prey. I kept my eyes forward. "You're not the child you once were. The arrogant, naive, reckless little girl has been replaced by you, a woman of great power and responsibility.

"It's quite funny, really. I had always recalled the day you stood up to me, that dinner party. I remember how you shook with adrenaline and fear. Today, you approach me with caution and hold yourself with dignity. You carry yourself with grace, and though you look fragile, you are a bomb that is ready to ignite at any second.

"I'm surprised that you haven't told Siddiqis about your little secret. I can tell that you two have spent quite a long time together, and I can tell you are on a mission. What I don't understand, and please feel free to explain this to me," he stopped right behind me and I felt his body heat too close. I resisted the urge to turn around. "Why would a pregnant woman agree to go anywhere outside of her castle when she knows of the risks involved?"

Zila stood up suddenly, eyes wide with surprise. "What?"

I closed my eyes, knowing what would happen next.

I heard Siddiqis drop something he must have been holding and heard him turn on his heel. Suddenly, in a flash, he was right in front of me.

I opened my eyes and regretted it.

He had a crazy look in his eyes and looked shocked. "You're with child?" He kept his tone low, but I heard the unbelief in his tone.

I lowered my eyes, a move I had rarely done. My cheeks blushed, and I absently felt my stomach. Then I looked up into Siddiqis's eyes. "Listen," I whispered.

Everyone was silent, and all that was heard was silence, then the strong beating of an infant's heart.

Siddiqis jumped back. "You've been with child all along?" he yelled. He looked more hurt than angry.

I didn't flinch; I had known this would be his response. "Yes," I mumbled.

Zila walked toward us and pushed Siddiqis away from me. "Do not shout at her, Siddiqis. You will upset the child!" She scowled at Siddiqis.

Lucas, now having said what he wanted to have said, circled around me till he was next to Zila. "How long is it till the child is ready?" He looked curious and less menacing, if that was even possible.

I gave it a thought. "I'm pretty sure in a few months. I haven't had it properly checked out. I found out a couple of days ago, really," I admitted.

Siddiqis wasn't done with his rage fit. "All along, you've been pregnant and you didn't say a thing to me!" He swiped a hand through his hair. "Oh god, how did Gustav even agree to this? How did any of your friends agree to this?" He went from a growling tone to a shout.

Zila tried to hush him, but Lucas spoke. "The better question to answer all those questions would be, do they know?" He spoke slowly and narrowed his icy grey eyes.

By now, I didn't look away; I had nothing to be ashamed about, I had realized. "Only a nurse and two others know."

"And I'm inferring that your husband isn't aware?" The look on my face answered his prediction. "Well, that does explain a lot. I'm sure no one sane would let a pregnant woman be alone with the Sinner, even if she is the Chosen Hybrid."

I went rigid. "You know of my title?"

Siddiqis interfered, now standing beside me. "And of mine?"

Lucas smirked. "Rumours. All confirmed when you two walked in. I felt your energy. It radiates through these very walls. Anyone with years of energy sensing can sniff you two out." He looked back down to my stomach. "Girl or boy? Or is it too early to know?"

I looked down as well and rubbed my stomach, as if to soothe the child. "A girl. She's aging fast. She has the blood of a vamp, hybrid, and dark angel in her. She's probably coming out in a few months."

"Why aren't you developing a bump?"

"I use special medication . . . why are you so curious of my child?" I asked, eyes narrowed.

Lucas laughed. "I'm actually just curious."

I nodded but kept my guard up.

Siddiqis went back to ranting. "I can't believe this. After all that we have been through. Even though we are linked, you didn't tell–"

"Pardon?" Lucas asked, his eyebrows rose. "You're what?"

I looked over at Siddiqis, who was glaring at me. "Well, we are linked. The current prophecy linked us together, and that's why we are going to the Prophecy Sisters. We need to break this bond," I explained.

Lucas was no longer smiling; he looked shocked. "You're going to summon the sisters? You two will die."

"We are hybrids. The sisters only listen to hybrids," I told him.

He nodded, but he looked slightly uncomfortable for some odd reason.

Siddiqis continued ranting. "Like I was saying, you didn't tell me that you are carrying another life force in you! Oh god, if Gustav knew about this, he'd kill me. No, all your friends would kill me." His voice boomed, and I refused to flinch.

"Siddiqis, just calm down–"

"You're pregnant, for God's sake, and you didn't even tell me! After everything we have been through! Even after I told you about Denis, my hope and son, you chose to just keep this–"

"Siddiqis!" I shouted, eyes wide.

There was a pause as Siddiqis then realized what he had said.

Lucas and Zila both turned their attention now to Siddiqis; both of them were stunned. "What did you just say?" Zila whispered.

Siddiqis looked ready to take back what he had said, but then his expression went stony and guarded. "I have a son. He's a year old, turning two in a month." He smiled softly. "His name is Denis Nrubrats."

Zila narrowed her eyes, hurt. "I have a grandson, and you didn't tell me?"

Siddiqis sneered. "I'm sorry. I was too busy being outlawed by you and your husband to tell you the news. I also did die, and there's no cell service in hell."

Zila wanted to say more, but Lucas cut her off. "You say this child's name is Denis Nrubrats?"

Siddiqis nodded slowly.

"Last time I recalled, your last name, sadly, is not Nrubrats. It's Starburn. So how dare you change his last name?" Lucas growled.

Siddiqis stepped forward, and I saw that he was actually taller than his father. "Let's get something straight. I was never part of this family in the first place. You tortured me and made my life a living hell. The only reason I stayed back was for my Razeil until you banished me from stepping foot back into this castle till my death." His eyes now glowed. "My child, my heir, will not bear the name that has brought misery upon myself and has caused fear in others. He deserves a normal life, one of joy and no despair.

"With my last name, he would carry a burden. I will not let him suffer the way my own father made me suffer!" Siddiqis shouted, and Zila flinched. "He carries my humanity. He is my life force. He is my son, and I will not make the same mistakes that you made with me! He will be loved, he will be strong, and I will not allow you to ruin his life before it has even begun!" The lights flickered, and the chandelier above swung.

Then without saying anything else, Siddiqis stomped out of the room, leaving us all dumbfounded.

# CHAPTER 21

## Long Talks

I SUCKED IN a breath, shaken by the sound of pure disgust in Siddiqis's words. I turned to Lucas and Zila; both stood still like statues and looked stunned. "Well, I guess that's my cue to leave."

I turned away, but then Zila caught my arm gently. "Can I go speak to him for a minute?"

I turned back to her, expecting the question to be for Lucas, but it was actually directed to me. "Are you sure? He doesn't seem to be in the mood for conversation–"

"I must. Please, may I?"

I knew she was pleading me, so I softened up. Zila was always kind to me. "All right."

Zila nodded a "Thank you" and rushed after Siddiqis, the doors closing behind her. Lucas and I stood eyeing each other cautiously.

I wasn't happy about being alone with Lucas, but there was no way I would show him that.

Finally, he spoke in a low voice. "How do you feel?"

"About becoming a mother? I'm not sure," I admitted. "It's . . . pleasant."

"No, not of that," Lucas said. "I meant, how do you feel about having to worry about your life and another's?" He gestured to my stomach. "If Siddiqis were to die, you would die. If you die, the child dies as well. You've got quite a problem on your hands, Kyra."

I shivered on the inside at the sound of my name rolling off his tongue. "I will protect my child at all cost. Even if it means having to make sure Siddiqis stays alive and well."

Lucas nodded, as though he had suspected my answer. "You always were noble. Ruthless nonetheless, but noble to a fault. I found it refreshing." He started to smirk, but then he frowned. "I still do not understand why you think fondly of Siddiqis, however."

"Siddiqis and I had a past together. It's in the past, though his mistakes have not been forgotten. I'm working with him because I must. That's all there is to it."

"No, that isn't just it. I see the protective shield you have around him. You care for him. No matter how many times you deny it, it is still the truth."

I considered it. "Maybe so. Maybe deep down, I do still care for Siddiqis. But that proves nothing. My lover is Gustav Deatheye. My love for him will outshine the darkest of nights."

"No need to be poetic, Princess. I understand."

"All right, but I have one question that you must answer. The answer will be between you and me."

"Ask on then."

"Why do you hate Siddiqis with such malice? He is your firstborn heir, yet you tortured him and banished him." I blurted out, wanting to know what had fuelled the violent actions he had done to Siddiqis.

Lucas exhaled with a sigh. "Siddiqis was destined to be my failure. I suppose any Demon king, especially one that is brothers with the Greatest Evil, will be content and pleased to have an heir that is told to be vile."

He looked over his shoulder at the swords that hung on the wall. "But when I left the Demon Realm, I wanted a normal hybrid son, not one that would rise higher than me or be wicked. The second Siddiqis came out of his mother, I looked into his eyes and saw . . ."

I waited, but he didn't go on. "What did you see?" I asked, curious.

He looked at me slowly, his eyes glassy as if he were witnessing it all over again. "I saw death. Chaos. Destruction. I saw Siddiqis rising up from the depths of the Demon Realms and wrecking everything. I saw pure evil, and at the same time, I saw an innocent child that I loathed. I tried to make Siddiqis softer at one point.

"But then when you and he were twelve, I went back to the Demon Realm because my brother had summoned me. Imagine my shock when I was told that Siddiqis, my own son, was to become the Sinner, the disgraced, and the death of those who cared of him.

"I had to do something. So after that day, I tortured him, hoping he would one day kill himself and prevent the prophecy from becoming true. But now I realize it only made him more ruthless."

He then did something that surprised me; he took both of my hands into his and looked at me with hopeful eyes. "After you and Siddiqis's link is severed, you must kill him. For your kingdom, your husband, your child, and for everyone's sake, you have to kill him. Give me your word you will do so, and I will do everything I can to keep your child as safe as possible. I will become your ally, and your child, when she is born, will be happy and safe. I swear to you I will make it happen, as long as I get your word that you will deliver my son to his death."

I was stunned, torn between what I felt and what I had to do. I knew my child would be in danger the second she breathes her first breath, that all my enemies will emerge from the shadows and come for her. I knew that killing Siddiqis would be best for everyone. But there was a part of me that wanted to scream that I wouldn't kill Siddiqis for my own need, that I still cared for him deeply despite all he had done.

I exhaled the breath I kept in and nodded. "I give you my word," I whispered, overwhelmed with emotions.

He smiled genuinely. "Thank you, Princess."

I stared over his shoulder at the swords, saying nothing. They were the Starburn family swords. Each at least once used in a great battle that the Starburn had won. It was a way of showing off trophies, but these trophies were stained with blood.

There were originally four of them, the sharpest for Lucas, the jeweled for Zila, the platinum for Siddiqis, and the ancient-looking sword for Razeil.

Now there were only three. Lucas's sword was above Zila's, with their names encrypted into the handle, while under Zila's sword, there was a space where Siddiqis's sword would've been, and under that was Razeil's sword with her name, birthday, and death day encrypted into the blade.

I curtsied to Lucas. "It's time for me to depart now. Until again, Your Majesty," I said politely.

Lucas grinned and bowed. "Until again, Chosen Hybrid."

I then turned away from him and walked out of the room, just as Zila emerged again. I curtsied to her. "I must go now. Until again, Your Highness."

Zila smiled warmly. "Farewell, Princess. We wish you good luck on your journey."

I nodded in thanks and exited the castle. As I walked out the front doors, I saw Siddiqis sitting on the edge of the fountain, looking sulky.

I walked toward him and then plopped down beside him. "At least no one got killed," I said, trying to lighten up the mood.

Siddiqis spoke, staring straight in front of him. "I'm taking you back to Xercus."

I scoffed. "I'd like to see you try."

Siddiqis suddenly blew; he shot up and loomed over me. "You don't get a single say in this! I've called Gustav, and he's expecting you back at Xercus, in your castle, where you will be safe!" he yelled.

I spoke calmly, trying to keep in the rising irritation and anger. "Siddiqis, I know that you're upset–"

"I'm furious, Kyra! Though it has been a few days, we've become a team, and you kept your pregnancy a secret from the people that matter the most to you! You could've at least told Gustav about the child, or Aries–"

"Aries already knew. He was against it at first but knew that I had to do this."

"Well, then, what about Gustav, huh? You have a commitment to him, don't you? The second I told Gustav about you, he started freaking out, saying how he should've known, how he couldn't believe you didn't tell him that you're pregnant with his child! He's the parent to your child as well, Kyra! He deserved to know!" He was now shouting at the top of his lungs.

I sat, staring up at him in dumbfounded silence. I had nothing to say; he was right, after all. Gustav and I were a team. My mind raced with a million thoughts, all saying I should've told him, I should've told him, I should've told him. A wall in my heart broke, and I didn't know I was crying until I felt the tears drop onto my hands. I began to sob and sob, covering my face with my hands, my shoulders shaking violently.

Siddiqis, seeing how far he had pushed me, immediately softened and went down on his knees in front of me and held my shoulders. "Hey, I'm sorry. I shouldn't have gone that far." He pulled my hands away from my face, but I kept my head down so that he wouldn't see my blotched face. "I understand where you're coming from. It's true he wouldn't let you go, but maybe that's not a bad thing.

"What if you fell? What if someone hurt you? What if you got killed? Kyra, if you died, it would be my fault. If something happens to you and your child . . . I wouldn't be able to live with myself. What you did was reckless. I'm taking you back to the castle, and you're going to stay there and I'll break the bond on my own. I'll bring the Prophecy Sisters to you if I have to. We are not going to lose you or that child. I'm not going to lose you."

I looked up slowly and saw that fierce, raw emotion in his eyes that I only saw a couple of times.

"Kyra, it's time that you stop rushing into danger and just stay at your castle. You need to rest." He stood up and then ran a hand through his hair. "I'll meet you in the Jeep."

As he walked away, I sat there, pondering on what to do. Siddiqis sounded so genuine, not evil and menacing. But did I really trust him? An image of Gustav popped into my mind, and I got into the Jeep, saying nothing.

"Time to go home, Kyra."

Home, I thought. Why do I get the feeling I shouldn't be going back there?

*****

Gustav was waiting in front of the castle at 6:00 p.m., sitting on the steps with his head in his hands. As soon as we pulled up, he looked up and ran toward us.

Siddiqis opened my door, and I stepped out, right into Gustav's arms. I took in his minty scent, his warmth, his racy heartbeat; I took all of him in.

Then he pulled away suddenly, looking both scared and cautious. "I'm sorry. Did I hug too tight or . . ."

"What?" I looked down at my stomach and realized what he was talking about. "Oh, no. It's all right. I'm fine. She's fine." I gestured to my stomach.

"She?" Gustav repeated. "We're having a daughter?"

I nodded, smiling.

He laughed and gave me another hug. "I'm so glad and relieved that you're back, Rumblen."

Siddiqis cleared his throat. "Well, I guess I'm headed back to find the Prophecy Sisters. See you in a few days." He nodded at Gustav, and to me he smiled sadly. "Farewell, Mrs. Deatheye and future mother." And with that, he climbed back into the Jeep without another word and took off, occasionally looking back through the rearview mirror at me.

I waved and then turned to Gustav, ready for a lecture. "Gustav—"

"Kyra, I'm not mad. I'm just upset. I wish you told me that we are going to have a child. And going on this trip while being pregnant? That was no doubt your worst idea yet, darling. But I understand why you went, and I'm more excited than hurt." His clear blue eyes bathed me in love and forgiveness.

I blinked a few times, letting it all sink in. "I'm sorry, Gustav," I whispered, feeling blessed to have such a loving husband and torn from keeping the baby a secret from him.

"It's all right. Just from now on, no more secrets. We are a team." He gave me a kiss, and then, arm in arm, we walked into the castle.

All my friends were waiting in the foyer. The second they saw me, they all ran toward me, congratulating the two of us on the pregnancy and on taking the path down parenthood. Even Stefan wished us well.

It all happened in a blur, and suddenly, I was whisked up the stairs and ushered under the soft blanket of my bed. Angela, who now had pulled the curtains closed, turned to me with tears of joy in her eyes and smiled. "It's great to have you back, Kyra. Get some rest." Then she left, shutting the door behind her.

But I couldn't sleep. How could I? The only thoughts in my mind were that Siddiqis now held the lives of my daughter and me and that he could die just trying to summon the sisters alone. Panic and fear froze me still, and I struggled to keep clam. I checked the time; it was 7:00 p.m. Time had gone by quickly, and Siddiqis would already have been on his way to the sisters, too far to come back and take me with him.

Sneak out, a sneaky thought whispered. Then in came thoughts that warned me not to do so, but that one sneaky thought grew louder and louder until it completely changed into a different thought altogether: Find Siddiqis.

I sat upright in an instant, my hands trembling. What's wrong with me? I thought, panicked. Without wanting to, I got out of bed and went into the walk-in closet. I tried stopping myself, but it was as if my body was no longer under my control. I pulled aside all the clothing, revealing a hidden door. I threw the door open and walked down the staircase it led me to, unable to resist the pull that had taken over.

There were several secret passageways through the castle that many didn't know, even Gustav. I had uncovered them all after finding one, and figured I should keep them a secret. They all led in one direction: outside toward the battlefield.

I finally threw open the door and was outside, hit by the smell of roses and the evening scent. It looked close to raining, and so I rushed toward the wooded area, remembering the secret portal that was there. I threw branches aside as I trudged through the woods, and finally, there it was: the portal. I tried fighting the unknown force that controlled me, but it was stronger. I was dragged toward the portal, and suddenly an image popped inside my mind: a cliff with a cave in the middle and Siddiqis climbing up to the cave and struggling.

    Realizing what was about to happen, I continued to struggle, but I was then pushed into the portal, disappearing in a quake of glimmering dust.

# CHAPTER 22

## The Sisters

I LANDED ON my feet, bending my knees to brace the fall. I looked around quickly, already knowing where I was: the Cursed Cave. The force that controlled me was gone, and I turned around just in time to see Siddiqis pull himself up onto the cave's opening.

When he saw me, he blinked a few times and then spoke in a low voice. "I swear, these hallucinations are so lifelike–"

"Siddiqis, it's me," I interrupted, looking over my shoulder at the cave.

He reached out to see if I was real. When he touched my arm, he pulled back as if I had electrocuted him. "Oh god. What are you doing here!" he shouted, his voice echoing.

I shook my head. "I have no clue. I was at the castle, and then I felt like something had taken over my body and then I went through a portal and here I am." I squinted at him. "How did you get here in one day?"

He narrowed his eyes. "Same way you did, through a portal that I made, which, mind you, took about half an hour. But I thought of the ground, not the cave, so I ended up at the bottom of the freaking cliff and had to climb up because my powers wouldn't allow me to turn into anything with wings!"

I turned away and peered into the large cavern. "I can't believe this is where we are supposed to summon the sisters."

"Kyra, you do realize that even if we get this bond lifted, Gustav is going to kill me because I decided not to bring you back again, right?"

I knew by his tone that he was running his hands through his hair; I didn't even have to turn around to know it.

"Well, the sooner we get this fixed, the sooner I can go back."

I began to walk into the cavern when Siddiqis grabbed my arm. "Wait." He knelt down in front of his bag that I saw he had brought and rummaged through it until he pulled out a small map. "This map will lead us to the right spot to summon the sisters. We need to do this before 8:00 p.m. or else we'll have to wait another day."

"Okay. Lead the way," I said, and from my weapons belt, I took out my moonstone, and with a quick chant, it lit up like a star in my hand.

Siddiqis did the same, and we headed inside the dark, damp cavern. It was darker than I had thought, but the moonstone gave off enough light so that we were able to see. It was a rather large cavern with damp stonewalls and a smooth stone floor. The faint dripping of water was deafening in the silent wake.

After walking for what seemed like fifteen minutes, we came to a part of the cavern that split into two tunnels.

Siddiqis looked down to the map and frowned. "This doesn't seem right."

"What is it?" I asked, looking down the left tunnel.

"There should be three tunnels, and the third tunnel will lead us to the Summoning Point, where we need to summon the sisters." He kept looking up at the two tunnels and back down to the map. "This makes absolutely no sense. We've been going the right way the whole time . . ."

"What if the tunnel . . . is here?"

"Kyra, I don't see a third tunnel."

"What if it's been hidden? What if we are supposed to see two, but really there are three?" I thought out loud.

"An illusion." He caught on.

"Yeah." I begun to feel the large space of rock in between the two tunnels, and my hand went through. I gasped, pulling back quickly. "Found it," I announced, satisfied as I turned to face Siddiqis.

He smiled and scoffed. "Wow. Good thing you came, I guess. But to be safe, I'll go in first."

I nodded and stepped aside, and he walked right into the wall and disappeared. I waited three seconds and then went through, feeling tingly. I emerged on the other side, right next to Siddiqis, and gasped. The tunnel was filled with crystals that lit up.

I muttered another spell, and the moonstone's light went out; Siddiqis did the same. We walked through, amazed at the amount of magic that it must've taken to light up all the crystals.

We turned the corner and entered a big open space. The ceiling was clear, and the moon was right above, meaning we were right on time. There was a stone table in the middle of the room, where lay everything we needed to summon the sisters.

Siddiqis smiled. "This is it, Kyra."

I nodded; a smile crept to my mouth. "Let's get started quickly."

We gathered around the stone table, and we looked through the history book on the sisters Siddiqis had brought along for information on summoning the sisters. When we found out what we had to do or say, I started lighting up the candles on the table and set them in a circle around us, while Siddiqis got salt and made a pentagram out of the salt on the stone floor. When we were ready, we both stepped into the pentagram, anxious and excited. We held hands like we did when summoning the Book of Prophecies.

I took in a deep breath and exhaled, feeling my eyes flash. "Ready?" I asked him, trying not to show how nervous I was.

He nodded, exhaling. "Ready."

We began chanting, our voice joining together in perfect harmony. "Two hybrids, both acting as one, summon the sisters of the great watchtowers. Ek oh tak lei boa!" We chanted this many times, and suddenly, the cave was illuminated with a great white light, and then as sudden as it came, the light was gone.

Siddiqis and I looked around and then let each other go.

He cleared his throat. "So . . . did it work?"

"Siddiqis, do you see the sisters anywhere?"

"No, but maybe it takes some time."

I checked my watch. "It's 8:01 p.m. We did the spell correctly, right?"

Siddiqis stepped out of the pentagram and picked up the open history book, peering at the spell. "Yeah, we did everything right."

I stepped out of the pentagram to his side. "Then why didn't it—"

Suddenly, all the candles' flames went brighter than before, and in the middle of the pentagram appeared two young ladies from thin air.

Siddiqis and I shrieked but quickly recovered from our shock, as the ladies looked our way.

They were both wearing dresses; one wore a white one, and the other wore a black one. They had an elegant feeling that came with them. Both were identical; they were twins. Both had the same perfectly curved lips, the same small nose, the same hair as black as the night sky, and the same skin that shone and sparkled. The only difference between the two was the colour of their eyes. Both had a haunting stare, but the one in black had grey eyes, like mine, and the girl in the white dress had golden eyes. They were supernaturally beautiful; Siddiqis and I were intrigued by their inhumanly looks.

"Hello, hybrids," they greeted in unison, creepily.

Siddiqis looked over at me and then at the two. "Um, hello."

"Make yourselves known, hybrids." The way they spoke was really disturbing; their voices were harmonious, one being light while the other being low. Yet, their voices echoed when they spoke.

I cleared my throat. "I am Kyra Rumblen Deatheye, eldest daughter of the deceased Count family and wife of Gustav Deatheye. I am the Chosen Hybrid."

Siddiqis found my hand and held it while he spoke. "And I am Siddiqis Starburn, eldest son of the Starburn family and the Sinner."

The golden-eyed girl smiled. "The Chosen Hybrid and the Sinner. What a surprise." Her tone was now friendly and easy-going.

The grey-eyed twin was expressionless, however. "What is it that you want, hybrids?" She seemed to be the darker of the two.

Siddiqis spoke with confidence that I somehow was unable to now find. "The current prophecy has linked Kyra and me together, but that hasn't been very helpful. And according to the prophecy, only the Sisters of the Prophecies can break our link."

The golden-eyed girl's smile turned into a smirked. "Yes, that is correct. I am Karma."

"And I am Death," said the other.

I finally found my voice. "We really need to break this link. You see, I'm—"

"Pregnant," Karma finished my sentence with a bright smile. "Yes, I do remember seeing that in a vision. You will have a lovely daughter." She motioned for us to step back into the pentagram, and we did, stopping in front of them. "You see, my sister must break the link. Only then will I be able to rewrite the prophecy." She turned to her sister, a slender hand on her shoulder. "Sister?"

Death walked in front of me, and in her hands appeared a dagger. "Are you ready, hybrid?"

I almost fell back.

Siddiqis caught me and hid me behind his body. "Whoa, whoa, whoa! I don't see how us dying will do anything but take us to our end."

Karma chuckled. "My dear Sinner, Death must do her part in order for me to do mine."

I gasped. "But I'm pregnant! If I die, my child dies!"

"No, Chosen Hybrid. Your child will not die, for she is the Dark Beauty, the immortal hybrid that will be bonded to my very own soul."

I gaped at her. The Dark Beauty was a legend of a hybrid that would be hated by many and loved by only a handful of people. She would carry the burden of killing those she kissed and would be the voice of Karma.

I had always thought it was just a silly old tale, but I had also thought the same about the Chosen Hybrid.

Siddiqis was shaking his head. "No way. That's impossible."

"Is it? Is it really, Sinner?" Death smirked. "It was said that the Chosen Hybrid and the Sinner were just fairy tales, was it not? If you two are them, then what else could be true, hmm?"

We were both silent for a long time.

Then I stepped out from behind Siddiqis and nodded numbly. "Okay. I'm ready."

Death grabbed my left shoulder with one hand and positioned the dagger over my heart. "Is this where your heart is?" she asked in a monotone voice.

I was confused for a minute, and I looked over at Karma to see her gesture at her eyes. Oh, she's blind, I realized, then remembering the history book, and looked down where the dagger was. "Um, yeah. That's where it is."

Death nodded. "All right. Now remember, this is going to hurt a lot for you." And without hesitation, she plunged the dagger right through my heart.

I gasped, eyes wide, as I looked down. I heard Siddiqis cry out and turned my head to see that he had also been stabbed.

Then I turned back to face Death to see her chanting words in a demonic language, and she released my shoulder, causing me to fall to me knees. Karma knelt down in front of me and kissed my forehead. "You will awaken soon, as well the Sinner. And though your heart shall stop, your child will remain alive in your womb, healthy and calm. Now sleep, child."

And so I plunged into a deep sleep as my heart beat two more times and then stopped.

# CHAPTER 23

## Aftermath

I GASPED FOR air, sucking in as much as I could get without choking on it. Each death hurt more every time; this one was excruciating. I struggled to my knees and then felt a hand on my shoulder.

I looked up to see Karma smiling down on me. "Welcome back, Chosen Hybrid."

"How long was I dead for?" I rasped.

She held out her other hand, and in her palm appeared a blood bag. She offered it to me, and I restrained myself from snatching it right out of her hands. I gently took it and bit into the plastic, drinking the blood slowly.

"You were out for about two hours. The Sinner recovered an hour before you and left right afterward."

"Siddiqis left?" I groaned. "I made a promise to end him right when the bond was broken. I must find him." I threw the now empty blood bag to the side in slight frustration.

Karma had a thoughtful look on her face. "Well, if it's any help, I heard him muttering about a child he needed to see. Possibly his heir."

"How do you know . . ." I paused, remembering whom I was speaking to. Of course she knew about Denis; the Prophecy Sisters knew everything. "Well, thank you very much for that piece of information, Karma."

She nodded, smiling. "Not a problem. My sister left after I had my vision of the next prophecy so that she may retrieve the Book of Prophecies so that we may write in the new prophecy."

I was curious. "What is the new prophecy, if you don't mind me asking?"

Karma smiled. "You are curious yet polite. That is why I shall tell you." She now had a wise look upon her face as she recited the new prophecy. "The Chosen Hybrid and the Sinner shall battle once more, and only one shall live." She paused. "I caution you to be careful, Chosen Hybrid. I did not see who will die or who will live, for only my sister can see such, and she will not reveal such to me. Your only luck, find the Sinner before he finds you."

I nodded, taking in all that I have learned, and I bid her goodbye. I took the history book and, within minutes, found myself running out of the cave, toward the edge of the cliff. I peered over the ledge just in time to see Siddiqis step through a portal he had created.

I was about to start climbing down when I remembered that the bond was broken; my powers were back. Grinning, I chanted a spell and took the form of a bat, flying down and straight through the portal, just as it closed behind me.

In a flash of light, I appeared right outside a small cottage and quickly hid in a tree, and I saw Siddiqis approach the cottage. I perched on a branch, watching curiously. I could tell we were in Possull, by the looks of it, though I had no idea which city. There wasn't a soul in sight, but I still used my bat hearing.

Siddiqis was banging on the front door. "Kylie, let me in!"

The door swung open, and standing in the doorway was a girl who looked to be eighteen years old. She wore a scowl on her face. "I told you never to come back here, Siddiqis."

"I'm here for my child."

"He's not here."

I saw Siddiqis's hands start to shake. "Where is he, Kylie?" he asked through gritted teeth.

She glared at him coldly. "I gave him to his grandparents."

"Okay, then tell me where your parents live."

"Not my parents. He's at your parent's castle."

I almost fell out of my tree.

Siddiqis went white as a ghost. "What?" he whispered in disbelief.

"That's right. I gave him to your parents. Your father came by and told me that he would be more than happy to take in his grandson and raise him as a Starburn. I never wanted a child. I thought I could take care of him, but I just couldn't. He's a freaking Starburn hybrid, and he freaked me out."

"You gave . . . my child . . . to my father!" Siddiqis screamed.

"I never wanted him in the first place! You told me it would be great, but all he brought was pain!" she screamed back.

Siddiqis, without saying anything, slapped her across the face. "How dare you do such a thing without even telling me?" he yelled, eyes blazing purple.

Kylie, now holding her sore cheek, stared up at him with sudden shock and fear. She was silent.

"Do you understand what you did? My father will kill him!" He turned on his heel and stormed away, running a hand through his hair.

I watched Kylie stare at him numbly and then slam the door shut.

Siddiqis was now holding his head, gripping his hair. "Oh god, why, why, why!" He punched the tree I was in, and it shook violently, causing me to lose my grip. I managed to turn back into my natural form and landed on my feet.

Siddiqis jumped back, startled by my sudden appearance. "What the hell!"

We stood there, eyeing each other. Then without a word, I turned back into a bat and took off.

Siddiqis yelled after me, but I didn't listen. Am I really going to do this? I asked myself as I headed toward the Starburn castle. Kidnapping was something I never thought about doing, but then again, Siddiqis needed to be brought down.

I arrived at the castle in a matter of minutes and flew up to every window I spotted, peering in each one.

Finally, I found him fast asleep in the tower where Siddiqis hid from his father before.

I broke through the window and changed back into myself. Looking around, I saw that it wasn't a good room to keep an infant in. It was clean, but there was only a single baby crib in the middle of the small room, where little Denis was fast asleep.

I went over to the crib and stared down in awe at Siddiqis's child.

He was flawless, with glowing tanned skin. He looked perfect–a small mouth, an adorable nose–and each breath he took caused his little chest to go up and down at a hypnotizing pace. He truly was a Starburn; all of them were hauntingly beautiful, even Lucas.

My eyes were glued on the infant, and then I realized I had little time until someone would find out I broke in. I quickly but gently picked up Denis, and as I was about to go out the window, I stopped. How the heck am I supposed to carry him in bat form? I looked around, panicked.

Then I remembered something my mother had taught me when I was younger. I put Denis back down into his crib and thought about how I was going to do this. I took in a deep breath, and closing my eyes, I envisioned wings coming out of my shoulder blade for a good five minutes.

Suddenly, I felt a rippling pain in my back, and in a second, massive grey wings came out of my shoulder blade, arched to the ceiling. I touched one with awe and grinned with satisfaction through this pain. It had worked.

I picked Denis up again and headed for the window. Just as I climbed onto the ledge, I looked down to see Denis peering up at me, wide awake and calm.

I stood there, rigid, waiting for the child to scream and get me caught. But he didn't do anything. He just stared up at me with fascination and curiosity.

What an odd child, I thought. Then I met his eyes and was transfixed by their depth. They were a dark blue, which looked close to being gray, but there was no mistake that they were blue. And they were filled with curiosity and life. They were calm yet stormy. This little infant stared up at me with amusement and fascination and looked like he knew what I was doing and was perfectly content with it.

I looked away only when I saw below me a portal was being opened. There was a flash, and then it disappeared, and standing in front of the castle was Siddiqis with a very pissed-off expression. I watched him run up to the castle doors and start banging, yelling for someone to open it before he broke it down.

I quickly flew out of the room with Denis in my arms and hid in a tree right in front of the castle, watching as Lucas opened the door and stood there, surprised to see Siddiqis. I listened to their conversation.

Lucas was staring at Siddiqis with an unreadable expression. "What do you want?"

"I want my child back now." Siddiqis seethed.

"He is a Starburn. You were planning on keeping my own grandson away from me. I think you can understand why I took him in."

"That was before. Now I want him to bear my last name."

"And why is that?"

"I was remembering the old stories Mother told me, like the stories of the Chosen Hybrid and the Sinner. I learned that Kyra's child will become the Dark Beauty, and if that's true, then my child will be the Destroyer, for I am the Sinner."

"Yes, I see that to be true. The Destroyer, being son of the Sinner, will be equal to the Dark Beauty. Though his heart will be one of good, his blood will be one of evil. He will be able to kill any who touches his blood or ingests it. That's what I remember from what I've been told."

"Yes, but you missed another detail. The Destroyer will be able to compel anyone but the Dark Beauty. And if he is able to do that, he can compel armies to work for me. He can compel people to even kill themselves." He grinned. "I need that child. He is my heir, and I am his rightful guardian."

"I will not allow you to take my grandson. Yes, you have thought out your plan, but it is not right for an infant. I am surprised, for before, you had claimed you wanted the child to be loved and to have morals, but what you speak of sounds like you plan on using this infant for your own needs. How are you to care for this child, hm?"

"I can take care of him better than you ever could."

"I've decided that for Denis, I will change my parenting ways. I looked into that child's eyes, and I saw what I look like to others. I saw what I could've done for you and what I didn't do. And I started to regret what I had done to you, but now I see that even if I hadn't hurt you, you would still be a selfish monster." His eyes flashed. "I will not let you have this child."

Siddiqis stared at his father with surprise, and I peered from the tree in awe. It was amazing how much this child could change people, including Lucas.

Siddiqis then narrowed his eyes. "At least let me see him one last time."

Lucas hesitantly opened the door wider and let Siddiqis in. I knew right then and there, if I didn't leave, I would get caught. So as soon as the door closed, I flew out of the tree and back to Xercus.

It took a long time to fly back, and by the time I got there, it was midnight. I finally reached the front door and banged on it hard.

I heard Gustav run up to the door, and he pulled it open. He glared at me, ignoring both the wings and the baby in my arms. "Kyra Rumblen Deatheye, you must stop sneaking off!" he yelled.

I stared at him, blinking. Then, I pulled my wings back into my shoulder blades and spoke calmly to him. "Gustav you need to let me in NOW."

That's when he looked down at the infant in my arms and gawked. "Whose child is this?" He seemed to have now forgotten his rage and was staring at Denis with a calculating expression.

I bit my lip. "Get everyone to come to the meeting room. That means all our friends, Aries, and Urani."

Sensing I had something important to discuss with everyone, he nodded and set out to gather everyone.

In a matter of minutes, the meeting room was full of people, and we all sat at the table; I stood at the head of it.

"Before I explain what will happen, you should know that I am sorry for running off. It was the stupid link with Siddiqis that drew me to him." I saw Gustav nod at the corner of my eyes. I launched into my story. "After performing a spell to summon the Prophecy Sisters, they showed up and told us that if we died at the hands of one of the sisters, the link would be severed. And when I asked what would happen to my child if I had died, I was told that my child is the Dark Beauty." At this, everyone gasped. I continued. "We severed the link, and Siddiqis took off right afterward.

"Siddiqis made love with a vampire a year ago, and they had a child, a little boy. Siddiqis wanted the child to be raised normally and not as a Starburn at first. But then, after hearing about my child being the Dark Beauty, he realized his child is the Destroyer, a hybrid that can compel anyone but the Dark Beauty. He wants to use his child to compel an army against us."

I held Denis in my arms and lifted him higher. "This is Siddiqis's only heir, Denis Starburn. I took him so that Siddiqis will be unable to use him. He could've screamed and got me caught for taking him, but like the legend says, he has a good heart. If we keep this child away from Siddiqis, we have a greater chance of winning this battle against him."

Everyone was silent.

Then Aries spoke. "Why don't we just kill him?"

Before anyone else could speak, I shook my head. "If a drop of his blood gets on your hands, you die, as the legend states. And he is only a child. I believe he can be different than his father."

"Kyra, do you really think it's a good idea to have an infant that can hypnotize any of us in the castle?" Angela asked, eyeing Denis cautiously.

"I know it's a crazy idea, but if I left the child, Siddiqis will have used him for his own cause." I looked down at the infant, and he smiled, reaching up to grab my lock of platinum hair. He grabbed it and giggled. I smiled as well. "See? He's just a baby."

Everyone stared at Denis as he contentedly started to babble.

Gustav then stood out of his seat and came to my side, peering down at the infant. He smiled a little. "He is just a baby, isn't he?"

He looked at me, eyes bluer than they had ever been. "We'll keep him until all this dies down. Right now, where's Siddiqis?"

"Last I saw him, he was going to get Denis, so at his castle in Possull. He knows that I know that he wants the child. Meaning, he may be on his way here."

Aleks now stood up. "Then let him come. We'll be ready."

Everyone chimed in, agreeing, and I looked down at Denis once again, wondering how much trouble this little infant was going to be for us. Little did we know, he was going to be a handful.

<br>

End of Book 2

To be continued.

Next Book<br>*A Destiny*

"Choices are made. Trust is broken. Love is dangerous."

"Haven't read the first book? Buy the first installment to the Chosen Hybrid Series to find out where Kyra started her epic journey!"

Printed in the United States
By Bookmasters